At 9:18 the last plane touched down on the *Akagi*'s flight deck and Nagumo immediately swung his ships around to a northeasterly heading and set fleet speed at 30 knots. The big Japanese carriers left churning wakes behind them as they pointed their bows northward. Below the flight decks a frantic struggle was going on to get the planes armed, fueled and readied for attack. But almost immediately enemy aircraft were sighted. Admiral Spruance had followed orders to "proceed southwesterly and attack enemy carriers," and his thunderbolts were soon to fall on the Japanese fleet.

For Nagumo and the Japanese fleet the magic spell was broken . . .

Also by Thaddeus V. Tuleja

TWILIGHT OF THE SEA GODS

CLIMAX AT MIDWAY
THADDEUS V. TULEJA

A JOVE BOOK

This Jove book contains the complete
text of the original hardcover edition.

CLIMAX AT MIDWAY

A Jove Book / published by arrangement with
W. W. Norton & Company, Inc.

PRINTING HISTORY
W. W. Norton edition published 1960
Jove edition / September 1983

ISBN: 0-515-07403-9

Jove books are published by The Berkley Publishing Group,
200 Madison Avenue, New York, N.Y. 10016.
The words "A JOVE BOOK" and the "J" with sunburst
are trademarks belonging to Jove Publications, Inc.

PRINTED IN THE UNITED STATES OF AMERICA

To My Wife

CONTENTS

Illustrations between pages 112 and 113

All photos are Official Photographs U.S. Navy, except one as credited.

Maps and Charts

~~~~~~~~~~

INTRODUCTION

WHEN THE idea for this book on the battle of Midway was accepted by the publisher a delivery date was agreed upon which, at the time, seemed within easy reach. As I got deeper into the research I discovered, much to my disappointment, that the task was more formidable than I had at first imagined. Battle reports were not always in agreement with one another; some details were uncovered only after a long and painstaking search through volumes of records, and unknown facts came to light after I had corresponded with or interviewed many key veterans of the battle.

All the official sources made available to me by the Navy Department were studied with care. I have assembled a valuable collection of letters from those veterans who were kind enough to answer my inquiry for information, and I also have notes taken during my interviews with various officers who were engaged in the battle. With this material in hand I began the story of that titanic sea fight, of the two fleets engaged in it, and of the thousands of American officers and men whose valor and devotion to duty transformed a potential defeat into a stirring victory.

A writer who extols the sea and the ships he has known and loved perhaps can be forgiven if, in spite of avowed objectivity, his favoritism shows through. Anyone who has served at sea knows that ships, like human beings, have living personalities. Some are "happy ships," or "good feeders," or simply "rust bucket," which even the most malcontented sailor would defend against ridicule by others. Ships may be personified with such affectionate titles as "Lady Lex," or "Sister Sara," but the character of each one is nothing more than the collective character of all the officers and men who man her and give her life. The *Yorktown,* which sank at Midway, was far more than a floating airfield. She was a person, and the officers and men who had been her crew before a Japanese torpedo took her life wept unashamedly as they stood on the decks of rescuing destroyers and watched her roll over and slip into the sea. And the valiant but tragic flight of Torpedo Squadron Eight from the carrier *Hornet* was no ordinary air operation against the enemy; it was an act of uncommon valor and heroism. The quiet courage of men under fire, the loneliness of command, the charity of the brave in the face of death are things which rarely appear in official battle reports.

This book, in its modest way, will attempt to tell the story of the battle of Midway, of the men who fought through the engagement, and of those who died in the struggle for victory. It cannot be the whole story: in any war there must always be unsung heroes and forgotten acts of courage.

Any decisive battle will lose its brilliance and historical

inevitability if it is studied merely as an isolated event. For that reason I have included some background material which will give the Battle of Midway its proper climactic quality in the flow of human events. History in its simplest form is a series of causes and effects, and it is often difficult to decide at what precise point in time an historical narrative ought to start. When did the long road to Pearl Harbor begin? To go back to 1854 for an answer might seem to be straining the point unduly; nevertheless, it was Commodore Perry's contact with sequestered Japan which changed that nation's historical destiny, brought her by a circuitous route to "Battleship Row" on the morning of 7 December, 1941, and led her six months later to the climax at Midway. What happened to the Japanese Fleet northwest of that lonely atoll on 4 June, 1942, was the beginning of the end, not the end of the beginning.

This book would probably never have been finished had it not been for the generous help of many naval people who assisted me in gathering information. I am grateful to Fleet Admiral Chester W. Nimitz, USN, who clarified for me the risks involved in his vital command decision to defend Midway when it was not known with absolute certainty that the Japanese attack was being directed there; to Admiral Frank Jack Fletcher, USN (Ret.), then Commander of Task Force Seventeen, who graciously received me in his Maryland home to discuss the battle; to Admiral Raymond A. Spruance, USN (Ret.), then Commander of Task Force Sixteen, whose several letters helped me to reconstruct a portion of the battle; and to his son, Captain Edward Spruance, USN, who described for me *Tambor's* predawn contact with part of the Japanese Fleet on 5 June; to Captain James S. Gray, Jr., USN, who was at the time of the engagement skipper of the *Enterprise's* Fighting Squadron Six, and who discussed with me in person and later recorded in writing the part his squadron played in the battle; to Captain E. D'H. Haskins, USN, then executive officer of the *Flying Fish*, who described his submarine's war patrol at the time the Midway battle was developing.

A special vote of thanks is due to Rear Admiral Ernest M. Eller, USN, (Ret.), Director of Naval History, and to his deputy, Captain F. Kent Loomis, USN, (Ret.), who put the war records of the Navy Department at my disposal, and to the staff members of the Navy Historical Records Section, who cheerfully helped me track down elusive bits of information; to Rear Admiral Maxwell F. Leslie, USN, (Ret.), who graciously prepared a full report for me of the battle as seen from Bombing Squadron Three, which he then commanded, and who was most generous in answering the many questions I raised in our long and pleasant correspondence; to Captain Paul A. Holmberg, USN, also of Bombing Squadron Three, who sent me a very elaborate account of the battle, and who discussed the action with me during one of my trips to Washington; to Mr. George Gay, only survivor of Torpedo Squadron Eight, who provided me with a great amount of material concerning the members of his ill-fated squadron and raised some points which threw new light on our generally accepted version of the battle.

I want to express my thanks to Rear Admiral W. G. Schindler, USN, for his account of the Japanese attack on the *Yorktown*. He was then Staff Gunnery Officer with Admiral Fletcher and witnessed the action from the carrier's bridge; and a special acknowledgement must go to Mr. Joseph H. Adams of Houston, Texas, who was then attached to Admiral Fletcher's staff as Communications Yeoman and who drafted for me a very full and dramatic description of the sinking of the *Yorktown* as he saw it happen. And to Father John L. Ryan, S.J., I wish to express my sincerest gratitude for extending to me the wonderful hospitality of Georgetown University during the many weeks of my research in Washington. Finally I would like to thank my two older sons, Tad and Ed, for thumbing through fourteen years of back issues of the *United States Naval Institute Proceedings* and tabbing them for whatever information they would yield on the Japanese Navy. I hope that I have not discouraged them from historical research.

I would also like to acknowledge my indebtedness to Devin-Adair Company for permission to quote from Andrieu d'Albas' book, *Death of a Navy;* to the *United States Naval Institute* for permission to use several passages from their book by Fuchida and Okumiya, *Midway, The Battle That Doomed Japan,* and to Mrs. John C. Waldron for permitting me to quote from her husband's last letter, which was written on the very eve of battle.

Every historian hopes that his analysis of past events will ring true, but I must assume that there will be some people who lived through the Battle of Midway, or who studied it from war reports, who will not necessarily agree with my narrative. Of course, I must accept full responsibility for the words I have written and the ideas I have expressed. Naming the people who helped me in the preparation of this book does not excuse me from any errors that may appear in it. I can only hope that in time it will prove to be as accurate as I have tried to make it.

T.V.T.

Saint Peter's College,
Jersey City, N.J.
15 September 1959.

CLIMAX AT MIDWAY

CHAPTER
1

~~~~~~

THE ROAD TO MIDWAY

*To robbery, slaughter, plunder, they give
the lying name of empire; where they
make a solitude they call it peace.*
TACITUS: *Agricola*

THE BATTLE OF MIDWAY, as the engagement came to be
called from the moment the first exultant battle reports were
drafted announcing an American victory, was only one of
many clashes between the Imperial Japanese Navy and the
United States Navy before the long Pacific struggle came to
an end. But the importance of Midway lies in the fact that
it was a decisive battle in the Pacific War, turning the tide
of the war and shattering the Japanese dream of invincibility. Not since 1592, when Japanese Admiral Hideyoshi
was soundly beaten by Korean Admiral Yi-sun, had Japan
known the meaning of defeat at sea.

Midway was a battle won by the underdog. It was a battle which might easily have been lost, since the United
States Navy, still suffering from the slaughter of Pearl Har-

bor six months before, was not able to assemble a fleet that could match the tremendous, three-pronged armada of Yamamoto.

The Japanese were counting not only on occupying a forward island base to strengthen their insular defense line, but also were bent on drawing the United States Navy into a sea battle which, it was hoped, would lead to its total destruction. The battle was a decisive reverse not merely because the United States Navy denied Midway to the Japanese invasion fleet, but also because this was accomplished with frightful destruction to the enemy's naval strength. All four carriers of Admiral Nagumo's Striking Force were sunk, along with one heavy cruiser of Admiral Kurita's Close Support Group. For this staggering victory, the United States Navy traded one carrier and one destroyer. It was a naval air battle, the second such battle in the history of sea warfare, in which the opposing surface fleets did not once sight each other; and the aircraft carrier came to prominence in naval power and thus altered the form of sea warfare in the Pacific.

Midway was more than a tactical victory with far-reaching strategic effects; it was also the end of almost a century of Japanese political expansion—an expansion that had begun shortly after the departure from Japan of Commodore Matthew Calbraith Perry in 1854, carrying a treaty which permitted American vessels to pick up supplies in Japan and opening the ports of Shimoda, Hakodate and later Yokohama to American trade. With the subsequent westernization of Japan, her expanding foreign trade buttressed her position in the economic world, and an astonishing economic revolution took place which transformed her from a feudal agricultural nation into an industrial power with a political and social structure part feudal, part modern. Her railroad and shipping lines were extended; factories were constructed across the land; and her shipyards built a navy that grew with her expansion.

Japan's warriors rather than her statesmen became the leaders of political life. Working under the spell of growing national power, they were prepared to defend their island empire and to expand it wherever possible. At intervals of ten years Japan fought three wars, dislodging the Chinese from Formosa and Korea, the Russians from Sakhalin and Manchuria, and the Germans from Shantung. Her first real challenge was with Russia, and her astounding victory in the Tsushima Strait in 1905 resulted in world recognition of Japan as a major power.

By the third decade of the twentieth century, Japan was mistress of the Far East. Her oceanic empire reached deep into the Pacific; German World War I losses gave her a mandate over the Marianas (except the large southern island of Guam, which was ceded to the United States in 1899), the Carolines, and the Marshalls, whose geographic center lay about 1300 sea miles south of Midway.

At the Washington Conference of 1921–22, called by Western statesmen to preserve the precarious peace of World War I and to regulate the naval strength of the great powers, Japan's ends were again admirably served. The conference finally settled on a 5-5-3 naval ratio for the United States, Great Britain and Japan. This ratio guaranteed Japan's national security against either Anglo-Saxon power singly, since it was generally agreed that neither the United States nor Great Britain could hope to defeat Japan in her own waters unless battle was joined with a fleet at least double that of the Japanese Navy.

In 1922 Japan signed the Nine Power Treaty in which the signatory nations agreed to "respect the sovereignty, the independence, and the territorial and administrative integrity of China," and to support "equal opportunity for the commerce and industry of all nations throughout the territory of China." But Japan signed the document with tongue in cheek. She waited until 1931, one year after the London Naval Conference, which had modified the old 5-5-3 capital ship ratio to read 3.25 for Japan, 5 for the United States and 5.2 for Great Britain, and then set out to conquer Manchuria, next driving southward toward the Great Wall of China. By 1935 Japan had brought devastation to the lands south of the Great Wall and simultaneously rounded out her aggressive Manchurian policy by buying up all Russian interests in the Chinese Eastern Railway. In the following year she withdrew from the 1930 London Naval Conference, thereby announcing to the world that her navy would no longer be restricted by treaties.

In 1937, when the rest of the world was preoccupied by Hitler's aggressions, Japan struck again. Peking, Tientsin, and Nanking fell in rapid succession; then Suchow, Canton and Hankow. By the end of 1938 organized resistance against Japan came to an end; but the Japanese continued their brutal and needless bombing of Chinese cities. During 1938 the United States sent several notes to Japan, protesting the bombing of defenseless civilians, insults to Americans in China, and Japan's interference with America's legitimate commercial rights. None of the notes had any effect.

Early in 1939 Japanese forces took the Chinese island of Hainan, and in July the United States gave notice of its intention to terminate its commercial treaty with Japan. In 1940, just four months after the European war began, Roosevelt asked for wartime emergency powers, higher taxes, and billions for defense; and in July of 1941 he froze Japanese assets in the United States. Tensions between the two nations were strained to the breaking point when, in September of 1941, the Japanese overran northern Indo-China.

A month earlier Prince Konoye, Japan's premier, had tried to arrange a meeting with President Roosevelt, but neither the President nor Secretary of State Cordell Hull was able to discern enough evidence of good will from Japan's opaque proposals and the idea of the meeting faded, toppling Konoye's ministry. In October General Tojo, the fiery Minister of War, succeeded Prince Konoye. Earlier he had refused to withdraw his troops from China to appease the United States. Military occupation, he argued, was necessary to preserve the peace.

Meanwhile Admiral Kichisaburo Nomura, Japan's ambassador to the United States, tried to restrain the war lords from plunging the country into war. He failed, as did his colleague Saburo Kurusu, who joined him in his hopeless mission. Hull's note of 26 November to the Japanese envoys was as inflexible a document as any statesman could compose: Japan was to withdraw from both China and Indo-China before American commercial restrictions would be removed. Tokyo then sent an encoded message to its embassy for relay to the State Department, which concluded:

"THE JAPANESE GOVERNMENT REGRETS TO HAVE TO NOTIFY HEREBY THE AMERICAN GOVERNMENT THAT IN VIEW OF THE ATTITUDE OF THE AMERICAN GOVERNMENT IT CANNOT BUT CONSIDER THAT IT IS IMPOSSIBLE TO REACH AN AGREEMENT THROUGH FURTHER NEGOTIATIONS."

Military and naval intelligence officers, who had accomplished the phenomenal feat of breaking the Japanese diplomatic code, read the message too. They also read the subsequent dispatch which instructed Nomura and Kurusu to deliver the Japanese note to Secretary Hull at 1:00 p.m. on 7 December, 1941, and then to destroy all coding machines and secret documents.

Vice Admiral Chuichi Nagumo, commanding the First Air Fleet, was then leading his carriers toward Hawaii. The attack on Pearl Harbor was scheduled to take place exactly twenty minutes after Nomura and Kurusu delivered their terminal note to the State Department. In Washington, diplomatic clerks were slow in preparing a smooth copy of the Tokyo note, and it was not until 2:20 in the afternoon that the Japanese envoys were received in Secretary Hull's office. By that time Pearl Harbor had been attacked. Among the military personnel, 3303 were dead, most of them from the Navy, and 1272 others were wounded.

The prearranged signal for the attack was a simple phrase, *Niitaka Yama Nobore* (Scale Mount Niitaka).

Nagumo had indeed reached the summit.

The Road to Midway

The blow at Pearl Harbor was not a total disaster for the United States Navy, but it was a heavy blow, and it was a necessity of military life that the burden of official guilt should fall upon the two commanders in Hawaii, Admiral Husband E. Kimmel and Lieutenant General Walter C. Short. They have been attacked and defended with vigor ever since. Fleet Admiral Ernest J. King blamed Kimmel for "a lack of superior judgment," while Fleet Admiral William F. Halsey called Short and Kimmel "military martyrs."

In any case the Pearl Harbor disaster meant the end of Kimmel's command of the Pacific Fleet, a command he had held since February of 1941. He was replaced by Rear Admiral Chester W. Nimitz, who was jumped over twenty-eight senior flag officers to be placed in the job. Although Nimitz accepted his new post with some reluctance, it was he who was to mastermind the vital Midway battle from his headquarters in Pearl Harbor and became, as much as any officer could become, indispensable to America's cause in the Pacific.

Kimmel's staff officers expected to be swept out of Pearl Harbor as soon as Admiral Nimitz arrived in Oahu, for in a way they were marked by the same misfortune as their former chief. Nimitz, however, arrived on 31 December with only a flag secretary, and after assembling Kimmel's old staff, he said, "I have every confidence in all the officers present. I would like you to stay on with me." Meeting Kimmel himself later, Nimitz shook his hand warmly. "You have my sympathy," he said, "the same thing could have happened to me."

Nimitz took over his command three-and-a-half weeks

after the Japanese strike. Pearl Harbor, with its half sunken ships and the stench of oil and burned-out hulks, impressed him profoundly with the enormous task that lay before him. "I have just assumed a great responsibility and obligation," he said solemnly, "which I shall do my utmost to discharge."

His first order from Washington was to defend at all costs an oceanic frontier which began on the eastern coast of Australia, moved northeastward through the Fijis, thence to Samoa where it turned northward, crossed the equator and ran on to Johnston Island, then northwestward to Midway. It was more than 4600 miles from Brisbane, its southern anchor, to Midway Atoll; beyond it to the west lay Guam and Wake, over whose shores now flew the flag of the Rising Sun. Japanese planes were poised on the coral runways of recently seized Tarawa and Makin in the Gilbert Islands, less than 2000 miles southwest of Oahu; and the Marshalls to the north of them, in Japanese hands since 1919, were already fortified.

Following the Pearl Harbor attack there was a veritable flood of Japanese troops and naval forces moving over the Pacific. These movements, tactically offensive, strategically defensive, were meant to smash all American, British, Dutch or Australian forces which might keep Japan from the oil she so desperately needed. Her fuel deficiency was perfectly understandable. With no wells of her own to speak of, Japan had had to buy oil abroad. In 1940 and 1941 she had been importing between thirty-seven and thirty-eight million barrels of oil, crude and refined, the bulk of it coming from the United States. This was far in excess of her normal consumption, but what she was not using domestically she was hoarding in thousands of storage tanks against the day when the war would come.

In the summer of 1941, when Japanese soldiers had over-run Indo-China, the American, British and Dutch governments had laid an oil embargo on Japan, which dealt Japanese sea power an especially heavy blow. Japan's most urgent military and naval objective, therefore, was to seize strategic oil fields near home waters and then encircle the area with an extensive defense line. To do this, Japanese war planners aimed at the early conquest of the Philippines and the Malay Peninsula, to be followed by the invasion of Sumatra, Java and the lesser Sunda Islands. The way would then be secure to take Borneo, chief of the Malaysian islands, with its rich oil fields. The Japanese could then push their defensive ring across the western Pacific.

Throughout December the news for the United States became steadily worse. The Japanese quickly neutralized potential bases for United States naval and air operations, in order to eliminate advanced staging areas from which counterattacks might be made. Guam was captured on 10 December, after two days of bombing; Wake, first attacked on the 8th, and heroically defended by a force of Marines, fell on December 23rd.

Japanese landings were made at Singora, Patani and Kota Bharu, and on the 19th they took Penang on Malaya's western shore. The Royal Navy, trying vainly to halt the disaster, lost two capital ships off the Malayan coast—the 35,000-ton battleship *Prince of Wales* and her 32,000-ton battle cruiser consort *Repulse*. On 17 December Japanese troops landed at Miri in the Sarawak section of Borneo, where the petroleum wells are rich and plentiful; and just before Christmas the capital of Sarawak fell, giving Japan the oil she so desperately needed. On Christmas Day the British base at Hong Kong, smashed from the air, attacked from land and sea, gave up the struggle.

The Japanese drove down the Malay Peninsula, and by 8 February 1942 invasion forces crossed the Johore Strait and landed on Singapore. On Sunday, February 15, the British surrendered Singapore unconditionally.

Meanwhile, the enemy was striking farther to the east. Toward the end of January, Japanese soldiers overran the beaches of New Britain, took Rabaul, and then reached out toward New Ireland to the north and Bougainville to the east. By the middle of February Palembang in northeastern Sumatra fell, and with it went the great oil wells of the East Indies. Soon Timor, most easterly of the Sunda Islands, brought the enemy to within 400 miles of Darwin, Australia, which was promptly evacuated as a naval base.

Java, too, was doomed, despite several heroic naval actions which took place between enemy units and a scattered fleet made up of the meager offerings of the American, British, Dutch and Australian navies. Early in March Java surrendered to the Japanese.

To the north in the Philippines there were further U.S. defeats. After devastating air strikes against Luzon, which crippled the U.S. air forces, the Japanese had crossed the Lingayen Gulf in December. Admiral Thomas H. Hart, Commander-in-Chief of the United States Asiatic Fleet, and General Douglas MacArthur could do nothing but fall back.

Manila was abandoned, and the retreat onto Bataan Peninsula followed. Early in April, American and Philippine troops under Major General Jonathan Wainwright evacuated Bataan and crossed over to Corregidor, which stood for five more weeks and surrendered to the Japanese in May.

Even before the Philippines fell the Japanese had blockaded China. Thailand; Burma's capital city of Rangoon; the Andaman Islands; and Mandalay, gateway to the Burma Road, were all in the hands of the Japanese. Early in April, Admiral Nagumo attacked Ceylon, concluding the first phase of his wartime cruising.

It is easy to understand why Admiral Nagumo contracted the "victory disease" which was spreading like an epidemic among Japan's high-ranking officers. During the four months which had passed since Pearl Harbor, months of Allied agony and Japanese jubilation, Nagumo had steamed across the Pacific, the South China Sea, the Bay of Bengal, and among the islands of Indonesia. He had immobilized the United States Pacific Fleet at Pearl Harbor, smashed two of Britain's capital ships, and sunk a number of destroyers and merchant ships. Add to this the damage he did to other vessels and to shore installations, and his score becomes formidable. What made this unimpeded slaughter even more grievous for the Americans and British was the fact that Nagumo accomplished his destruction without the loss of a major ship.

CHAPTER
2

~~~~~~~~

MIDWAY MUST FALL

I have never looked upon the United States as a potential enemy.
ADMIRAL ISOROKU YAMAMOTO

THEIR SWIFT and sanguine sweep across the Asian seas, from Pearl Harbor to Trincomalee, proved to the Japanese that their operational time table had indeed been wisely conceived, and naval planners were encouraged to forego the stage of consolidation which would have normally followed in the wake of Japan's victories. Therefore, instead of strengthening their defense lines, they decided that it was necessary to speed up their push eastward.

A preliminary plan to take Midway had already been drawn up by Admiral Isoroku Yamamoto, Commander in Chief of the Japanese Combined Fleet, early in April. Yamamoto wanted badly to strike at Midway, for he believed that such a blow would force the United States Fleet into a decisive sea battle. He was especially anxious to demolish Nimitz's aircraft carriers, for these had escaped the attack on ·

Pearl Harbor. With American naval air strength eliminated, Yamamoto could then bring his own carrier planes and his powerful guns to bear on the rest of the helpless American Fleet. Thus Admiral Nimitz's last defensive weapon in the Pacific would be destroyed and the ocean from Tokyo to Pearl Harbor, from the Aleutians to New Caledonia, would become a Japanese lake.

Nonetheless, there was an element of desperation in Yamamoto's plan. The Japanese admiral knew that America's industrial potential, already stepped up for war, would soon be able to make up the naval losses suffered at Pearl Harbor. Therefore, he decided to strike soon.

Isoroku Yamamoto, loved and revered by his own navy as he was hated and maligned by ours, was one of Japan's ablest naval commanders. Wartime propaganda described him as a hater of all things American since early childhood; and stated that he lived with only one purpose in mind, which was to dictate peace terms to the United States in the White House. The postwar period has put him in a more favorable light and has shown that much of the abuse heaped upon him during the war years was undeserved.

Yamamoto was regarded by many United States naval officers as a clever tactician with a high level of intelligence and an alert and active mind. An American naval officer who knew him personally believed that Yamamoto, who was an accomplished bridge player and a champion at Japanese chess, "possessed more brains than any other Japanese in the High Command." It was no secret that he wanted to develop strong carrier-based air power; it was through his efforts and those of his associates that the Japanese Imperial

Navy managed to have ten aircraft carriers in commission when the Pacific war began in December, 1941. The United States Navy, through no fault of its own, had only half that number, with only three of them in the Pacific.

Early in 1941 Yamamoto, influenced by the rapid deterioration of United States-Japanese relations, had argued that his country could have no hope of winning a war against America unless the United States Fleet based at Hawaii was destroyed. It followed that the most effective destruction could be achieved only by a surprise attack which would guarantee a heavy concentration of American warships in the relatively confined area of Pearl Harbor. Thus Admiral Yamamoto set in motion the staff work which was to lead to Combined Fleet's Secret Operation Order No. 1—to drive England and the United States from Greater East Asia.

Postwar histories, memoirs and interrogations show that some Japanese leaders, including Yamamoto himself, were not pleased with the Tripartite Pact of September, 1940, which linked Japan's military destiny with that of Adolf Hitler and Mussolini. Nor did they welcome a war with the United States, as did Japan's army leaders. In the days before Tojo's tyranny Yamamoto said to Premier Konoye, "If you tell me that it is necessary that we fight, then in the first six months to a year of war against the United States and England I will run wild, and I will show you an uninterrupted succession of victories." But he added solemnly, "I must also tell you that, should the war be prolonged for two or three years, I have no confidence in our ultimate victory." Once committed, however, Yamamoto and his associates did all they could to bring victory to Japan.

Despite this, it is difficult to read into Yamamoto's character a persistent, burning hatred for "all things American." The famous Japanese broadcast which carried Yamamoto's alleged boast about dictating the peace treaty within the walls of the White House was, in fact, a cunning distortion of a letter he wrote in January, 1941, to a Japanese friend. In that letter he said:

"Should hostilities once break out between Japan and the United States, it is not enough that we take Guam and the Philippines, nor even Hawaii and San Francisco. We would have to march into Washington and sign the treaty in the White House. I wonder if our politicians, who speak so lightly of a Japanese-American war, have confidence as to the outcome and are prepared to make the necessary sacrifices?" [1]

This was no magniloquent flourish, no insolent boast. Yamamoto's words carried with them a feeling of final doom, and it was perhaps that sense of ultimate tragedy which was to exert a subtle influence on his later tactical considerations.

The enormous operational tasks which lay before the Japanese Navy as its seagoing forces were gathering in a rich harvest of oil forced naval strategists to reexamine the urgent problem of future operations. Yamamoto strongly favored an advance to the east toward Midway. He based his decision on some very practical considerations. Vice Admiral William F. ("Bull") Halsey, was already poking holes in Japan's defense line. The Marshalls, for example, were hit on the first of February, followed a few days later by an air strike on diminutive Marcus Island, which lay some 960 miles southeast of Japan's coastline. Later an attack was

31

launched against eastern New Guinea, and in the following month a strike was mounted against Wake.

Early in April the Japanese Navy began a frustrating debate over Yamamoto's plans to seize Midway Island. On one side of the debate were those officers who felt that the Midway venture was far too hazardous; that there was no guarantee that Nimitz would risk his limited and weak naval forces in defending the atoll, as Yamamoto hoped he would; nor was there any real assurance that the occupation of Midway, assuming it could be done, would alarm the United States enough to bring about peace negotiations, as some of Japan's leaders were thinking. The proper places to strike, the anti-Midway clique insisted, were New Caledonia, Fiji and Samoa. This would close off the eastern flank of Australia and give Japan control of the southwest Pacific.

On the other side of the table were the Midway partisans, who wanted to draw the American Fleet into the ordeal of a decisive sea battle; and off on the sidelines—but not silent— were the supporters of an inexorable sweep westward toward Ceylon. So there were at least three basic plans on the long table, each with its champions, each with its peculiar risks. The selection of one of these plans had to be made quickly, but it was not the deliberate judgment of Japanese strategists which brought the naval debate to a close.

In San Francisco on the first of April, 1942, sixteen Army B-25's, two-engined, twin-ruddered, tricycled bombers, recently arrived from Sacramento, were hoisted aboard the United States aircraft carrier *Hornet*, Captain Marc A. Mitscher commanding. The bulky aircraft, which had never been designed for carrier launchings, were under the command of Lieutenant Colonel James H. Doolittle. During midmorning of the following day, the *Hornet,* accompanied by the cruisers *Nashville* and *Vincennes,* the tanker *Cimarron* and a division of destroyers, headed out to sea. The *Hornet* looked like a plane barge with her cargo of bombers clustered on her after flight deck, their wings projecting over the carrier's sides. The operation was a tight secret, and not until the force was heading westward in cruising formation did Mitscher switch on the loudspeaker and announce:

"This is the Captain speaking. We are carrying the Army bombers close to the coast of Japan for the bombing of Tokyo."

There was a burst of cheering from the crew. Mitscher, gladdened by this display of enthusiasm, was later able to note in his action report that "morale reached a new high, there to remain until the attack was launched. . . ."

Steadily the *Hornet* and her consorts steamed westward. On the 8th the carrier *Enterprise,* wearing the three-starred flag of Vice Admiral William F. Halsey, Jr., along with her own units, pulled away from Pearl Harbor and set a northwesterly course. On the 13th the two forces sighted each other and became united as Task Force Sixteen, under the command of Halsey, who now had two carriers, four cruisers (Rear Admiral Raymond A. Spruance), two divisions of destroyers and two fleet oilers. Since all of *Hornet's* own planes had been struck below to make room for Doolittle's bombers, the *Enterprise,* commanded by Captain George D. Murray, had to provide continuous combat air patrols for both carriers.

For the next few days Halsey's fleet held its westerly

course. On the 17th the carriers and cruisers were refueled. The tankers and destroyers were then detached, and the *Enterprise* and *Hornet*, protected only by combat air patrols and the 6- and 8-inch guns of Spruance's cruisers, began their full-speed dash to the launching area.

It was Halsey's intention to bring Doolittle to within 500 miles of the coast of Japan, from whence the Army pilots could mount a night attack on the Japanese capital and then fly on across the Sea of Japan to Chinese airfields. However, circumstances forced him to change this plan. Before dawn on the 18th, Halsey's radar picked up unidentified targets ahead. He waited until dawn and then launched several search planes. Before long the reconnaissance pilots sighted an enemy picket vessel bobbing on the choppy sea, and believed that they in turn had been sighted by the Japanese. Although the cruiser *Nashville* sank the unlucky patrol craft, Admiral Halsey realized that he had lost his most valuable asset—surprise. His force was still about 150 miles away from the proposed launching position, and if he attempted to reach it he would expose his two carriers to a certain attack by Japanese land-based planes. If he launched immediately, Doolittle and his airmen would not only have to attack Tokyo during daylight hours but also might never reach the Chinese airfields because of the additional flying distance.

Halsey and Doolittle weighed the prevailing risks against the military and psychological value of dropping a load of bombs on Tokyo's industry. There was little hesitation. After an exchange of signals, both men agreed that an attack on the Japanese capital, even in daylight, outweighed all other considerations. From the bridge of his flagship Halsey gave the order to launch planes, and signalled:

"To Colonel Doolittle and his gallant command good luck and God bless you."

Spindrift swept over the *Hornet's* ramp and an 18-knot wind whistled along the flight deck. Doolittle's plane lifted into the air, and the other planes followed without a mishap. By 8:30 they were all winging toward Japan, while Halsey was steaming at 24 knots eastward.

Three of the bombers were instructed to hit Kobe, Osaka and Nagoya, all to the southwest of Tokyo. The rest, coming in low, reached the Japanese capital about noon and made runs on munitions works, steel factories and power plants. Fires broke out, buildings collapsed, and Japanese gunners, taken by surprise, pumped an ineffective enfilade of flak into the air.

The planes departed as suddenly as they had come, leaving Tokyo stunned, confused and temporarily crippled. One plane touched down in Russia, the rest either landed safely or crashed in widely scattered places. Nine men did not survive the heroic flight. One died making a parachute jump; four drowned; another died in a Japanese prison camp; and three others—Second Lieutenants Dean Hallmark and William Farrow, and Sergeant Harold Spatz—were convicted of "inhuman acts" by a vengeful Japanese court and shot to death.

The Tokyo raid, which President Roosevelt announced had been launched from "Shangri-La," threw Japan's High Command into frantic activity. The Japanese picket vessel which had sighted Task Force Sixteen on the morning of the

18th had radioed its sighting to Japan before it was sunk, just as Halsey had suspected. However, the Japanese were at first unable to believe that the American carriers could possibly have launched a flight of heavy land-based bombers. Some naval officers thought that the planes had come from Midway,[2] which lies almost 2300 sea miles eastward of Tokyo. Others, taking the excessive range into account, came to the conclusion that the United States Navy somehow had developed a method for launching land bombers from a carrier's flight deck.[3]

Yamamoto was deeply shocked by the air attack. His beloved homeland, which he had tried to protect against just such a raid, had been rudely assaulted, resulting in a considerable loss of face for himself and the entire Japanese Navy. And when it was learned from captured American airmen that the attack indeed had been launched from a carrier, Yamamoto resolved to put an end to debate over the proposed Midway operation. All pending operational plans were either postponed or scrapped, and all former opponents of the Midway venture, sobered by the raid's sudden destruction, fell into line with Yamamoto.

Less than two weeks after Doolittle soared over Japan, "Operation MI" was ready for approval by the Naval General Staff. The plan included, in addition to the occupation of Midway, the capture of key positions in the Aleutians. Yamamoto was confident of Japanese naval superiority and believed that a thrust toward Midway would certainly force Nimitz to commit all his available ships to the defense of the island. This would lead inevitably to the great fleet action for which the Japanese Navy had been training for several years. With the United States Pacific Fleet sunk, Midway and some of the Aleutian Islands occupied, and Hawaii and Alaska threatened, American statesmen might be receptive to peace overtures. It was a very long shot, but Yamamoto was willing to take the gamble.

In the early part of May his staff officers, most of them hypnotized by the myth of Japanese invincibility, worked up a series of comprehensive war games, in an attempt to estimate the expected damage to Japanese forces at Midway. While they were thus engaged, a unique sea battle was being fought in the broad stretches of the Coral Sea.

According to earlier plans, Vice Admiral Shigeyoshi Inouye, commanding Japan's Fourth Fleet, was to make a stab at Tulagi in the Solomon chain, and then strike at Port Moresby on the Papuan peninsula, both operations to follow an assault in March on Lae and Salamaua on the northern end of New Guinea. However, Yamamoto learned that an American carrier force was operating near this area and decided to postpone the attacks until Inouye's fleet could be buttressed with additional cruisers and carriers. Toward the end of April the Fourth Fleet was joined by the light carrier *Shoho*, plus two fleet carriers, *Zuikaku* and *Shokaku*, and two cruisers from Admiral Nagumo's command. Inouye had no time to waste, for the carriers and cruisers loaned to him were scheduled to play a part in the Midway assault.

Quickly the two invasion forces were assembled. One, commanded by Rear Admiral Kiyohide Shima, was to strike at Tulagi, garrisoned by a small detachment of Australians; the other, led by Rear Admiral Sadamichi Kajioka, was to invade Port Moresby, which was, in General MacArthur's over-all strategy, essential to the defense of Australia. These forces were to be shielded by a covering group commanded by Vice Admiral Aritomo Goto and composed of the *Shoho*, the four heavy cruisers *Aoba*, *Furutaka*, *Kako* and *Kinugasa*, and a lone destroyer; plus a carrier striking force built around the carriers *Zuikaku* and *Shokaku*, and including two heavy cruisers, *Haguro* and *Myoko*, and six destroyers. This force was under the command of Vice Admiral Takeo Takagi.

While Tulagi and Port Moresby were being seized, a support group comprising the seaplane carrier *Kamikawa Maru*, the light cruisers *Tatsuta* and *Tenryu*, and three gunboats under Rear Admiral Kuninori Marumo was to set up an air base in the Louisiade Archipelago, a cluster of islands and reefs whose geographic center lies about two hundred sea miles eastsoutheast of New Guinea's eastern promontory.

Admiral Shima steamed out of Rabaul, headed southeast into the Solomon Sea, then swung northeast. On Sunday morning, 3 May, he invaded Florida Island, putting Tulagi in Japanese hands. The principal target of Operation MO, the capture of Port Moresby, was to follow a few days later. On the 4th Kajioka's invasion force, numbering about a dozen army and navy troop transports, slipped out of Rabaul and headed south.

But the Coral Sea venture was no secret to intelligence officers of the United States Navy, who had been collecting a rich harvest of information from Japan's leaky communication channels. Admiral Nimitz knew that the Japanese Navy was planning something in the Solomons and he had been able even to circle "3 May" as the date when operations would begin. The capture of Tulagi, of course, simply confirmed his estimate of the enemy's intention, by which time he had already set up his own strategy.

This involved Rear Admiral Frank Jack Fletcher who at the time was cruising in the Coral Sea, flying his flag from the mast of the carrier *Yorktown*. His force was screened by three cruisers, *Astoria, Chester* and *Portland,* and he was joined by Rear Admiral Aubrey Fitch's *Lexington* group, over which he assumed command as Commander Task Force Seventeen. At its full strength this force included the two 20,000-ton aircraft carriers, eight cruisers, thirteen destroyers, and two fleet tankers.

Admiral Fletcher, who had just celebrated his fifty-sixth birthday on 29 April, was no stranger to the Pacific, having been attached to the Pacific Fleet in 1909, and returning to the Asiatic Station again in 1922. When war broke out in the Pacific, Admiral Fletcher was in command of Cruiser Division Six, and was later named Commander Cruisers, Pacific Fleet. In February he had directed air strikes against Jaluit, Makin and Mili in the Marshall-Gilbert Islands; and in March he joined Vice Admiral Wilson Brown in a carrier strike on Lae and Salamaua which took the Japanese by surprise.

On the day following the capture of Tulagi, Fletcher was joined by the cruiser force of Rear Admiral J. C. Crace, Royal Navy, who headed a mixed command consisting of the American cruiser *Chicago,* the *Australia* and *Hobart* of the Australian Navy, and the destroyers *Perkins* and *Walke* of Destroyer Division Nine. In the middle of February Crace had met and conferred with Admiral Brown at sea, learning from the American admiral that he intended to use Crace's squadron as an advance screen, or attacking force. Fletcher saw no reason to change this policy.

Admiral Inouye rather expected Nimitz to contest the invasion of Port Moresby once it got underway, and if an American force entered the Coral Sea he hoped to meet it between the fleets of Goto and Takagi. Goto's ships were pushing sharply southward through Bougainville and Choiseul and were to cruise around the southern approaches to New Georgia, protecting the Port Moresby invaders. Takagi, steaming in Goto's wake, was to pass north of the Solomons. Therefore, no matter how Fletcher approached the Coral Sea, north or south of the Solomons, there would be Japanese naval planes waiting for him. With these defenses readied, Kajioka, escorting his convoy of troops, would swing around the Papuan peninsula and take Port Moresby.

Admiral Fletcher, having filled his tanks from the oiler *Neosho,* headed for a launching position west of Rennell Island to bomb and strafe the Japanese forces just landed at Tulagi. He made this move with only his own force, since Admiral Fitch was then taking on fuel and could not immediately join him. Beating northward at 27 knots, Fletcher speared through a wide belt of dirty weather. When he reached his launching position early in the morning of the 4th, he found clear skies and immediately flew off a flight of torpedo planes and dive bombers. A few minutes after 8 o'clock Tulagi was hit. Japanese troops scattered as the bombs fell. Trucks disintegrated in a flash of fire, and black smoke rolled out over the harbor, where Japanese transports were coming under torpedo attack. It took some time before the stunned Japanese were able to man their antiaircraft guns and fire at the retreating planes. Two more strikes were launched during the day while a small flock of Wildcat fighters buzzed over the *Yorktown* to protect her against enemy attack.

The yield from this vicious bombing of the Tulagi beachhead was disappointing—only a number of small vessels were sunk and an old destroyer crippled—but the attack boosted the morale of Fletcher and his men. It also informed Inouye and his admirals that an American carrier force had entered the Coral Sea. Hoping to simplify Yamamoto's impending Midway operation, Takagi drove his carriers hard to the south in an effort to trap Fletcher.

For the time being, however, Fletcher eluded the Japanese admiral. After the last plane touched down on the *Yorktown's* flight deck, he cut through the pass between Rennell and San Cristobal and then headed south to join Fitch, whom he met on the morning of the 5th, some 360 miles south of Tulagi. Believing that the Port Moresby invasion fleet would then be underway, he swung his force around to a westnorthwesterly heading to get in the vicinity of the Jomard Passage in the Louisiades, through which Kajioka would undoubtedly lead his long line of invasion transports. With the *Yorktown* group supported now by Fitch and Crace, Fletcher plotted his next move. At about the same time Takagi, who had been steaming at high speed on a southeasterly course along the northern fringe of the Solomons, swung around San Cristobal and headed into the Coral Sea on a westerly course. Meanwhile Goto, low on fuel, took some at Shortland, south of Bougainville, and weighed anchor once more in the morning of the 6th, heading southwestward for the Jomard Passage. About two hours later he was bombed by American B-17's flying out of Australia, but received no damage. Soon other American planes sighted Kajioka's southbound force, and Admiral Inouye knew that two of his fleets had been spotted. That same morning Takagi, having long since passed Guadalcanal on his starboard hand, had turned his force to the south, not knowing that the westbound Fletcher would thus be crossing his bow. At midnight, each unaware of the other's presence, the two admirals were just sixty miles apart, with Fletcher to the southwest of Takagi.

At dawn on the 7th, while Fletcher was nearing his launching position far to the westward, Takagi sent off search planes to the south, on the lookout for American carriers. An hour and a half later a Japanese pilot sighted the *Neosho* and her destroyer consort *Sims*, both of which had been sent south to a future rendezvous. Immediately the pilot (apparently nearsighted, since the *Neosho* was an oiler), reported the presence of a carrier and an escorting cruiser. Takagi ordered, "Launch planes for attack!" and less than thirty minutes later *Neosho* and *Sims* were being bombed. Neither ship had a chance. The *Sims* sank first. The *Neosho*, sending up clouds of black smoke, drifted for several days and was then scuttled.

While this attack was developing, Fletcher was some 150 miles to the south of Jomard Passage. At this point he changed course for the north. He felt that a carrier duel was imminent and since he wanted above all to frustrate the invasion of Port Moresby, he sent Crace's cruisers on a westerly course to rip into Kajioka's transports. For this Fletcher was later criticized, presumably because he divided his forces, and especially since Crace's antiaircraft fire was now lost to him. Admiral Crace, who no longer had any air cover, felt nonetheless that Fletcher was correct in his judgment, for the advantages to be gained by possibly intercepting Kajioka's invasion ships in the Jomard Passage far outweighed other considerations, and the retention of Port Moresby by the Allies was worth much more than the safety of the carriers. These evaluations were identical with Fletcher's.[4]

As it happened, Crace did not meet Kajioka but was himself vigorously bombed by the Japanese in the afternoon. His own skillful maneuvering, aided generously by the inaccurate marksmanship of the Japanese bombardiers, enabled him to escape the attack without a single ship being hit.

Meanwhile, Admiral Fletcher's morning search had spotted the small support group commanded by Admiral Marumo but had erroneously reported it as a carrier force. Quickly Fletcher moved into position for what he believed was to be an attack on Takagi's carriers. His planes, however, discovered Goto's ships instead and concentrated their attack on the *Shoho*. The light carrier was overwhelmed by the *Yorktown's* and *Lexington's* air power, and five minutes later she slipped into the sea, carrying about five hundred of her crew to the bottom.[5] The sinking of the *Shoho* left the Japanese invasion transports without air cover, at the cost of only a few planes to Fletcher, but he was disappointed that in following a false scent he had missed Takagi's two carriers.

At Rabaul, Admiral Inouye, now aware of Fletcher's approach and alarmed by the sudden appearance of Crace's cruisers west of the Jomard Passage, decided to move the troop-laden transports temporarily out of harm's way. Accordingly, Kajioka was ordered to reverse course until Fletcher's force was smashed. This change in the Japanese time table was made in the morning, before the sinking of the *Shoho* and Crace's remarkable escape from the bombing attack. Both incidents seemed to confirm the wisdom of Inouye's hesitant policy. Kajioka's retreating invasion fleet continued northward toward Rabaul, from whence it had steamed so confidently several days before. The temporary retreat became a permanent one and the Japanese Navy, accustomed to victories, was thwarted for the first time in the war.

Fletcher, of course, did not know about Inouye's enfeebling decision and therefore he moved westward, expecting Kajioka to glide through the Jomard Passage sometime in the morning of the 8th. In the meantime Takagi, trying desperately to locate Fletcher, was sending off flights of bombers and torpedo planes from the *Zuikaku* and *Shokaku*. Toward evening these pilots, failing to find Fletcher, turned back, jettisoning their bombs and torpedoes on the way. In the darkness they sighted the wakes of carriers beneath them and came down to make their routine landing approach from astern. Suddenly the pilots recognized the carriers as American! Frantically they gunned their engines and winged over, but before they were able to duck into the night shadows, an American combat air patrol pounced on them and sent several crashing into the sea.

During the night Fletcher changed course to the south-west, still in search of Takagi. Early in the morning of the 8th, patrol planes from both forces were in the air. At 8:15 one of Fletcher's pilots reported the sighting of Takagi's carriers. A few minutes later Takagi had reports on Fletcher, and all four carriers—*Yorktown* and *Lexington,* washed in the brilliant light of the morning sun; *Zuikaku* and *Shokaku,* partially concealed by clouds—were spotting planes for a huge air strike. The two admirals were then about 175 miles apart, with Fletcher to the southwest. Takagi launched 121 aircraft, Fletcher 122, and the air groups, enroute to their opposing carriers, passed each other in flight. It was the beginning of a new and strange kind of warfare.

The *Shokaku's* combat air patrol tried to beat off the attacking dive bombers and torpedo planes, but the U.S. Navy pilots dove in relentlessly, and soon the Japanese carrier was wreathed in smoke, her forward deck ripped open, her bulkheads blistering from the heat of burning gasoline. The *Zuikaku,* hiding beneath low clouds, escaped the fury of the attack.

At about the same time, the Japanese pilots were attacking Fletcher, who had no cloud cover for his carriers. With their backs to the sun they dove in. The *Yorktown* pulled to port, then twisted to starboard in an attempt to avoid the bombs and torpedoes. Toward the end of the attack the *Yorktown* was finally struck with an 800-pound bomb which tore through her flight deck and detonated deep inside her hull, killing and wounding a great many of her crew. Damage control parties leaped into action, isolated the fires, and soon put them out, and the *Yorktown* succeeded in avoiding further damage.

The *Lexington* was not so lucky. Caught in a crossfire of torpedoes, she was struck twice on her port side and then took bomb hits on her flight deck and stack. Smoke rolled over her bridge as flames drove the fire fighters back. The officers and men were devoted to "Lady Lex" and put forth a tremendous effort to save her. By noon it seemed as if their devotion was going to be rewarded: her fires were almost out, her flooding under control, she was able to steam at reduced speed, and her list was trimmed enough to allow limited flight operations.[6]

Then at 12:47 there was a thunderous explosion deep inside the ship which shook her violently from keel to masthead. Fresh gasoline fires spread rapidly below decks; communication lines were severed; ammunition detonated, and officers and men, caught in the violence of successive blasts, were blown up with the wreckage. The *Lexington* still was able to recover her planes from the strike against Takagi's carriers, and it was not until late in the afternoon that Admiral Fitch and Captain Sherman had to admit that their gallant ship was beyond hope. Her fires were now out of control and clouds of smoke and sparks poured from her hull. Sherman gave the order to abandon ship, and when all hands were free he swung down a life line, the last man to leave. Admiral Fitch transferred his flag to the cruiser *Minneapolis*. At about 8 o'clock that evening the *Lexington* slipped under the waves, as a mighty blast shook her frames.

The battle of the Coral Sea was over.

The loss of the *Lexington* was costly, especially since Admiral Nimitz was now aware that he would soon have to meet Yamamoto's eastward drive. At best he would be able to count on the availability of three carriers: *Enterprise, Hornet,* and possibly the *Yorktown,* if she could be repaired in time. Yamamoto had at least the four fleet carriers of Admiral Nagumo's force. He had also hoped to use Takagi's carriers, but the *Zuikaku,* having lost many planes in the Coral Sea engagement, did not have sufficient replacements when Yamamoto moved out to hit Midway; and the *Shokaku* needed extensive repairs.[7] Neither ship sortied for the strike at Midway, and therefore Nagumo's carrier strength was reduced by one-third on the eve of the great battle.

After trading the *Lexington* for the diminutive *Shoho,* Fletcher was determined to even the score; he was, however, satisfied that the enemy had not taken strategically valuable Port Moresby. The action apparently did not shake the Japanese belief in their own invincibility, and they prepared for their attack on Midway with supreme confidence.

CHAPTER
3

~~~~~~~~~

THE FLEETS SAIL OUT

*For if things turn out as I anticipate, and
we beat them at sea, then we shall have
kept your Isthmus free from the barbar-
ian, and they will have advanced no
further than Attica. . . .*
HERODOTUS: *Persian Wars*

MIDWAY, A LONELY ATOLL resting in the broad wastes of the
Pacific westnorthwest of Honolulu, was formally claimed by
the United States in 1867, eight years after it was presumably
discovered by an American sea captain. In 1903 President
Theodore Roosevelt placed Midway under the control of
the Navy, in which year it was also to become a vital link in
the cable chain joining the Philippines with the Hawaiian
Islands. Garrisoned with a small detachment of Marines, it
became a valuable sentinel for Pearl Harbor. In 1935 the first
Pan American clipper whirred up to the seaplane ramps
which the airline had constructed off Sand Island, the larger
of the two islets which make up Midway Atoll. The smaller
one, Eastern Island, a few years later was to be leveled off

into a landing strip for land-based planes.

Civilian travelers deplaning at Midway before the war saw islands of green brush and brilliant white sand set at the lower end of a lagoon ringed by reefs and the sparkling fringe of breaking surf. Sometimes a gray-hulled naval vessel swung at anchor off shore, while a red dredge scooped out a ship's channel in the foul ground between Sand and Eastern Islands. Both islands were literally covered with scaevoli shrubs, or dwarf magnolia, which sprouts glossy leaves like mountain laurel; and everywhere there was the "gooney" bird, a comic dancer of the albatross family, which covers the island with eggs during the laying season. The offshore waters teemed with tropical fish, and beyond Welles Harbor, which nature had etched out of the shoaling northwest of Sand Island, the fin of a shark might break the sun-flecked water and then disappear again.

Peacetime visitors were lodged in a one-story brown hotel whose many-awninged windows added a note of dubious elegance to the atoll; and laborers who volunteered for work on Midway found little more than hard work, a tropical sun, flocks of raucous sea birds, sand, and the eternal sea, stretching more than eleven hundred miles southeastward toward Oahu and over twenty-one hundred more in the other direction toward Tokyo. Nor was there much leg room on the islands: Sand was barely two miles long, Eastern a little more than one. But in June of 1942 this desolate atoll became the crossroads of two national destinies.

Admiral Yamamoto's orders to his fleet were elementary and ambitious:

1. In early June the main strength of Combined Fleet will capture Midway, and a part of its strength will seize the western Aleutians.

2. After completion of these operations, most of the battleship strength will return to the homeland and stand by, while the remainder of the Midway invasion naval forces will assemble at Truk to resume operations early in July for the capture of strategic points in New Caledonia and the Fiji Islands.

3. The Nagumo Force will then carry out air strikes against Sydney and other points on the southeast coast of Australia.

4. Following the above, the Nagumo Force and other forces assigned to the New Caledonia-Fiji Islands operations will reassemble at Truk for replenishment. Sometime after the beginning of August, operations will be launched against Johnston Island and Hawaii, employing the full strength of the Combined Fleet.[1]

Behind these official phrases were other significant objectives in Yamamoto's orders. The deliberate thrust toward the Aleutians, designed to throw Nimitz off balance, was also supposed to gain, even for a limited time, an outlying observation post in the dreary northern Pacific. The move toward Midway, on the other hand, which was to give Japan control of the strategic atoll, was supposed to end in a decisive battle in which the United States Pacific Fleet would be destroyed. Then the Japanese Fleet, following a pause for replenishments and repairs, would proceed for the strike against New Caledonia, Fiji and Samoa.

The whole scheme, when simplified, resembled the old single wing fullback spinner play often seen on college football fields. The tailback (Aleutian Invasion Force), after pretending to take the ball from the spinning fullback, sweeps wide around to his left with an armful of air, thus pulling the opposing team off balance. Meanwhile the fullback (Midway Invasion Force), having completed the spin, crashes hard off his own tackle with the ball in his arms and races for the goal line.

Considering the naval power available to him, Yamamoto's plan had reasonably good chances of success, but the strategists of Japan's Combined Fleet were, for the most part, a rather conservative lot who found it hard to adjust to changing times. They still lived in an age when the battleship, with its air of invincibility, made up the main power of a fleet, and because of this the aircraft carrier, already the most important naval weapon of the day, was cast in a supporting role. Had Yamamoto used his own powerful fleet to give gunfire support to those carriers attacking Midway, he might have carried away the victory he so desperately coveted.

On board the giant battleship *Yamato*, bearing Japan's ancient name, Combined Fleet staff officers worked out the last details of the Midway invasion. While they were busy with this, Japanese intelligence officers, hoping to determine with sufficient accuracy the total strength Nimitz would be able to throw into Midway's defense, had been collecting a mass of information, some of it sound, much of it spurious. Their final evaluation of American naval strength in the Pacific was as follows: [2]

Type of Ships	Japanese Estimate	Actual
Aircraft Carriers	2 to 3	3
Special Carriers	2 to 3	0
Battleships	2	0

Type of Ships	Japanese Estimate	Actual
Heavy Cruisers	4 to 5	7
Light Cruisers	3 to 4	1
Very Light Cruisers	4	0
Destroyers	30	14
Submarines	25	25

The disparity between the estimated and actual figures shows that Admiral Nimitz was even worse off than the Japanese expected him to be, and to counter this very modest force Yamamoto assembled one of the most prodigious displays of naval power in modern times, including ten battleships, eight aircraft carriers, twenty-four heavy and light cruisers, seventy destroyers, fifteen submarines, eighteen fleet tankers, and about forty transports, supply ships, tenders, minesweepers, patrol craft, submarine chasers, and minelayers—185 ships in all. From the decks of his carriers and the airstrips of Aur and Wotje, Kwajalein, Wake and Jaluit, Yamamoto was ready to launch 352 Zero fighters, 105 dive bombers, 162 torpedo planes, twenty-four fighter seaplanes, eight scout planes, ten land bombers and twenty-four flying boats, a total of 685 aircraft. This imposing sea and air armada was divided into six tactical fleets: the Main Force; the First Carrier Striking Force; the Midway Invasion Force; the Northern (Aleutians) Force; the Advance Submarine Force; and the Shore-based Air Force. Yamamoto was to ride with the Main Force, flying his flag from the *Yamato*, Japan's 63,000-ton battleship, whose main battery of 18-inch guns could fire a broadside of thirteen tons of steel. The First Carrier Striking Force, including carriers *Akagi, Kaga, Hiryu* and

Soryu, was commanded by Vice Admiral Chuichi Nagumo, whose planes had pulverized Pearl Harbor. Vice Admiral Nobutake Kondo, whose Second Fleet had spent a fruitless week at sea trying to catch Halsey after the Doolittle raid on Tokyo, commanded the Midway Invasion Force; the Aleutians Force was under Vice Admiral Moshiro Hosogaya; and Vice Admirals Komatsu and Tsukahara headed the submarine and air forces respectively. While in immediate command of the Main Force, Admiral Yamamoto was also Commander-in-Chief of the entire operation, a gigantic undertaking which mobilized seven vice admirals, eleven rear admirals and tens of thousands of officers and men.

Japan's powerful First Carrier Striking Force, after moving into a position some 250 miles to the northwest of Midway on 4 June, was to pommel the atoll with bombs, destroy its defenses and decimate its air strength. On the following day, while the pre-invasion air assault continued, a Seaplane Tender Group, commanded by Rear Admiral Ruitaro Fujita, was to occupy diminutive Kure Island, situated about 55 miles westnorthwest of Midway. Fujita, whose modest force consisted of a small carrier, a seaplane tender, a destroyer and a troop-carrying patrol vessel was to convert the island into a seaplane base and give support to the major landings which were to take place at Midway on the following day.

It was expected that by 6 June, after three days of murderous attack, the Midway defenders—if there were any of them left—would not be able to oppose invasion. Landings were then to take place, with 1,500 troops stabbing at Sand Island and 1,000 more storming the beaches of Eastern. Two construction battalions were to stand in readiness to follow in the wake of the assault waves and restore the operational status of Midway. As the assault got underway, Admiral Kurita's four heavy cruisers and two destroyers were to close the beaches and support the landings, while Admiral Kondo, with two battleships and four heavy cruisers, was to protect the flank of the invasion from the southwest.

Yamamoto held tenaciously to his belief that Nimitz would not rouse himself until after the landings were made, and that is why he planned to lay an extensive trap to the west of Midway into which it was hoped the United States Pacific Fleet would steam. He intended to position his own Main Force of three battleships, a light carrier, one light cruiser, two seaplane carriers, nine destroyers and two tankers about 600 miles to the northwest of Midway. Admiral Nagumo was to place himself about 300 miles to the east of Yamamoto's Main Force. His four carriers, all of which had been with Nagumo on 7 December, 1941, were supported by two battleships, two heavy cruisers, one light cruiser, a dozen destroyers and five tankers. About 500 miles north of Yamamoto was to be the Guard Force of Vice Admiral Shiro Takasu. This force, originally assigned to screen the Aleutians Operation, consisted of four battleships, two light cruisers, twelve destroyers and two tankers. About 300 miles to the east of Takasu was to be located the Second Carrier Striking Force of Rear Admiral Kakuji Kakuta, consisting of two carriers (one of them light), two heavy cruisers, three destroyers and one tanker.

If Admiral Nimitz, assembling his fleet at Oahu, was taken in by Yamamoto's Aleutian feint and sent his limited forces far to the northwest, Kakuta's search planes most likely would find them and stage an immediate air attack. Meanwhile, Takasu, bringing up the rear with his battleships, would rush in to support Kakuta's air strikes and bring any surviving American ships under the fire of his long-ranged guns. Should Nimitz's forces show up anywhere between Midway and Kakuta's carriers, then it would be Nagumo's mission to drive in for the kill, with Yamamoto's battleships moving in to deliver the *coup de grâce*.

But it was also anticipated that the American forces might try to move more directly toward Midway. Oahu lies over 1100 sea miles eastsoutheast of Midway Atoll. Between these two geographic points is a long and irregular chain of small islands, broad banks and coral reefs. No fleet commander, looking for a fight, would be inclined to hug the northern or southern fringe of this treacherous string of foul ground, for if the enemy's forces surprised him here, his freedom of movement might become greatly restricted. In defending Midway, however, circumstances might force Nimitz into taking some quick risks, such as sending his fleet along the northern or southern edge of this insular chain. Yamamoto was determined to block that possibility. Beginning just north of Gardner Pinnacles, which lies about halfway between Midway and Oahu, Yamamoto's staff officers drafted a line tending in a northeasterly direction for about 240 miles. A submarine squadron was assigned to patrol along this line and intercept any American force that crossed it. If Nimitz sent his ships to the south of the Hawaiian chain, they would have to cross a similar submarine patrol line stretching north and south for about the same distance. To intercept any American naval units steaming in the northerly latitudes of the Aleutians, a third but shorter submarine patrol line was established, its northern terminus fixed about 160 miles southward of Unalaska Island. And finally, from the Japanese-held islands to the south Yamamoto would direct his shore-based aircraft over the broad wastes of the Pacific in search of the American Fleet.

Yamamoto's grand strategy was now complete, and he proposed, after the operation was put in motion, to hold his forces at their designated stations for one week in battle readiness. He could afford to be patient. By this time Midway would have fallen and a desperate Nimitz would have to accept the unequal challenge of a fleet action which could end only in total disaster for the United States Navy in the Pacific.

It was true that Admiral Nimitz was in a desperate plight. A single act of bad judgment, one military blunder, and he would put not only his fleet but the whole Pacific war effort in jeopardy. His reputation was at stake, too, for an American defeat at Midway would have undoubtedly led to the loss of his Pacific command. But Nimitz had monumental patience and optimism. When he took over command of the Pacific Fleet after Pearl Harbor, he found "too much pessimism" at the war-scarred Hawaiian naval base. Nor was he shaken by a disillusioned public which asked caustically what the Navy was doing while the Japanese Fleet steamed everywhere with impunity. Unruffled, Nimitz uttered a simple Hawaiian phrase, *hoomanawanui*—be patient.

Admiral Nimitz was desperately short of ships; the *Lexington* was resting on the bottom of the ocean, and the *Yorktown*, after the pounding she had taken in the Coral Sea, was returning to Pearl Harbor for repairs. The defense line he was

committed to hold was fearfully long, stretching from the
Coral Sea northward over 4000 nautical miles to the fog-
bound Aleutians. And even had he been able to match Yamamoto ship for ship, or nearly so, Nimitz would have had to
wait for the Japanese admiral to tip his hand before he could
parry the first thrust. But Nimitz had a magical weapon which
the incautious Japanese unwittingly leased to him—their own
porous naval communication system.

It would be wrong to assume that Nimitz, sitting at his
desk at Pearl Harbor, was able to read every order that Yamamoto issued to his fleet. Wartime encoded radio traffic is
a highly complicated affair, and every fleet carries a great
many coding systems, each of which is altered periodically as
a precautionary measure against compromise; but the volume
of radio traffic from Japanese warships was laboriously collected and catalogued by naval intelligence officers attached
to Nimitz's staff. The repetition of call signs of various Japanese ships and naval commands previously identified, the
type of codes used, and the length and frequency of messages
warned Nimitz at an early date that Yamamoto was preparing
for a major movement of his fleet. United States submarines
operating in hostile waters at periscope depth were able to
bring back other scraps of information about Japanese ship
movements which fitted into the big jigsaw puzzle being assembled at Pearl Harbor. And so it was that by April intelligence personnel were able to hazard a guess that Midway
was probably the plum Yamamoto was after.

Yet this evaluation was not watertight and incontestable.
After Pearl Harbor there were few Japanese codes that could
be read with the same ease and accuracy with which Ameri-

can intelligence officers had formerly been reading "purple." Therefore, there were still many gaps in the puzzle and it would take a man of great fortitude and courage to put his finger on Midway Atoll and say confidently, "They will strike here!" The task was particularly trying for Nimitz. His own chief in Washington, Admiral King, believed that the Japanese assault was being aimed at Oahu, not Midway. But just before the battle was joined, naval intelligence tricked the Japanese into giving themselves away.

In their radio communications the Japanese never named Midway, but rather referred to the atoll simply as "AF." From the American point of view the big question was this: Does "AF" mean Midway, or does it mean Hawaii? Or possibly some other place? To find the answer, Pearl Harbor sent out an encoded message, instructing Midway to send back a fake plain language despatch, announcing that the atoll's fresh-water distillation machinery had broken down. Dutifully Midway transmitted the requested message, which could be picked up in the clear by anyone who cared to listen, including Japanese monitors. Pearl Harbor's intelligence officers waited. Then, after a couple of days, they intercepted a Japanese radio message broadcasting the fact that "AF" was low on water.

This information, as valuable as it was, did not inspire Nimitz's strategy; it merely confirmed it. As early as 2 May he had assembled key officers of his staff and had flown with them to Midway, where he imparted his estimate of the situation to Navy Commander Cyril T. Simard and Marine Corps Lieutenant Colonel Harold Shannon. Admiral Nimitz, who had celebrated his fifty-seventh birthday on 24 February, spent the better part of a hot day hiking all over the island, climbing into numerous dugouts and inspecting defensive installations. At the end of his exhausting tour, he turned to Shannon, in charge of the atoll's ground defenses, and asked him what further equipment he felt he required in order to beat off a Japanese invasion. Shannon pondered the question. Then he enumerated a long list of supplies and equipment. Nimitz asked further: "If I get you all these things you say you need, then can you hold Midway against a major amphibious assault?"

"Yes, sir!" Shannon replied confidently.[3]

As soon as Nimitz got back to Pearl Harbor he began assembling the matériel listed by Shannon, and by the middle of May it began to arrive at Midway—antiaircraft guns, dive bombers and fighters, tanks and infantry reinforcements. The role which Midway was to play in the forthcoming battle was now clear. If Yamamoto's initial air strikes succeeded in pulverizing the island's defenses, the possibility of a successful invasion would be increased. Therefore, the island's air strength, including Army, Navy and Marine Corps planes, was to seek out Yamamoto's aircraft carriers and bomb and strafe their flight decks. If this failed to reduce or eliminate the invasion threat, then the island's secondary line of defense was to be brought into play—barbed wire entanglements, offshore mines and gunfire. Many of the mines were ingeniously fashioned from sealed sewer pipes and ammunition boxes packed with dynamite and nails and each marked with a prominent bull's eye so that it could be detonated by rifle fire from the shore.

About two weeks after his surprise inspection of Midway,

Admiral Nimitz came to another decision he had been considering. Intelligence sources had indicated that the Japanese strike against the Aleutians was actually a ruse, but Nimitz was not willing to leave his far northern flank completely unguarded and so organized a force of two heavy and three light cruisers and a screen of ten destroyers, placing them under the command of Rear Admiral Robert A. Theobald. The mission of this force was to harass the enemy in the north while Nimitz reserved the bulk of his striking power for the protection of Midway.

At the moment Nimitz had a critical shortage of carriers, the one ship type which was to perform a decisive function in the coming encounter. Shortly after Doolittle's raid on Tokyo, Halsey had pushed Task Force Sixteen toward the Coral Sea, hoping to bolster Fletcher's force in those remote waters, but time had run out on him and he missed that earlier carrier battle. Quickly he swung around and headed for Pearl Harbor, arriving during the last week of May. His arrival gave Nimitz two carriers, *Enterprise* and *Hornet,* and for the time being that was all he had. On the 27th, though, the day after Halsey's arrival, Admiral Fletcher steamed into Pearl Harbor with his battered flagship *Yorktown.* There seemed to be little hope that she could be patched up in time to sortie with the other two. The 800-pound Japanese bomb that had ripped through her flight deck had stabbed its way deep inside the ship. Her bulkheads were twisted out of shape and her decks were blistered and blackened from the intense fires that had followed the crippling blast. Repairs were bound to tie her up in a drydock for many weeks, and one flag officer, considering the time that normally would be required to clear away her fire-scarred wreckage, patch up her leaks and rebuild her decks and bulkheads, estimated that some three months would pass before the *Yorktown* was in fighting trim once more. But Nimitz needed her and orders went out to repair her with anything on hand.

As soon as the *Yorktown* glided into the drydock, an army of shipfitters and machinists crawled through the ship's internal wound. Showers of sparks cascaded down her ladders as crumbled bulkheads were cut away; limp cables were ripped out and new ones were threaded through the ship, and in the machine shops ashore, crews of workmen labored feverishly fashioning new parts for the battered carrier. The work went on with heroic determination. There was no rest; each man worked as if he personally shared in the *Yorktown's* destiny. One shift followed another and the pace never slackened. By the afternoon of the 29th, just two days after the *Yorktown* had limped into Pearl Harbor, a miracle had happened. Nimitz had his third carrier.

He was also able to muster eight cruisers, fourteen destroyers, twenty-five submarines and a number of fleet tankers; and Midway itself, nesting bombers and fighters on its runways, would act as an unsinkable carrier. He had no battleships available, but since Yamamoto did not use his own wisely the shortage did not in the long run affect Nimitz's tactical position. Fortunately, then, it did not matter that American estimates of Japanese battleship strength were seriously in error. It was believed that Yamamoto would use only two to four such ships, while in fact his battleship superiority was overwhelming. Pre-battle estimates of the enemy's naval strength were as follows: [4]

61

Type of Ships	United States Estimate	Actual
Battleships	2 to 4	11
Aircraft Carriers	4 to 5	5
Heavy Cruisers	8 to 9	10
Light Cruisers	0	6
Destroyers	16 to 24	49
Submarines	8 to 12	16

Differences between estimated and actual figures for light cruisers and destroyers, had they been disclosed before the battle, might have given Admiral Nimitz some very anxious moments. It was fortunate for the U.S. that the striking force of these ships, along with that of the ponderous battleships, was squandered miserably, a fact not known until after the war.

Admiral Halsey was the logical flag officer to take Nimitz's fleet to sea, but illness overtook him and with reluctance he entered the Naval hospital at Pearl Harbor, leaving Task Force Sixteen without a commander. However, he stalled the medical officer long enough for a quick conference with Admiral Nimitz to discuss an immediate successor. His recommendation went to Rear Admiral Raymond A. Spruance, who had up to then commanded the cruiser force under Halsey. Nimitz concurred in the choice and Spruance was picked for the job, taking over Halsey's highly efficient staff. Admiral Fletcher was still in command of Task Force Seventeen, flying his flag from the mast of the recently reclaimed *Yorktown*. This gave him, because of his seniority, over-all command of the fleet but left both carriers of Task Force Sixteen under Spruance, who flew his flag, as Halsey had done, from the *Enterprise*.

Spruance possessed an inexhaustible vitality and superb intelligence, which are the ingredients of superior leadership. At the time of his appointment he was only a little more than a month away from his fifty-sixth birthday, and the long years of naval service since his graduation from Annapolis in 1906 had been spent in the usual run of sea and shore billets. In the late 1920's he was sent to the Naval War College in Newport, Rhode Island, for study, and this was followed by a tour of duty in the Office of Naval Intelligence. In 1931, and again in 1935, he returned to the Naval War College as a member of the Staff, and then, in 1938, received his first important sea command—the 33,000-ton battleship *Mississippi*. He was in a sense a "battleship sailor," but his thinking was flexible and he was always ready to consider new tactical concepts. Intense and single-minded of purpose, Spruance's virtues as a tactician were not lost on his seniors, and in 1941, as a Rear Admiral, he was given command of Cruiser Division Five, which operated with Halsey. This command showed in itself the trust the Navy Department had placed in him. While supporting Halsey's carriers in those early raids on the Marshalls, Wake and Marcus, Spruance quite naturally was expected to assume command of the entire force in the unhappy event that Halsey was killed.

The unending flood of war literature (to which Spruance made scarcely any contributions, since he refused to be interviewed by correspondents) often characterized him as an aloof, intense individual possessing a slide-rule brain. A truer picture emerges when this one-sided version is viewed against Spruance's own distaste for publicity. He aspired to no laurels; public clamor irked him.

Although he was himself rigidly abstemious in the use of tobacco and alcohol, he occasionally mixed cocktails for his friends. His strict physical regimen was supplemented by long walks which became famous in the naval service. On one occasion an old classmate of his, Rear Admiral Charles A. Dunn, agreed to accompany Spruance on a hike around the hills of Oahu. For hours Spruance set the pace with long and deliberate strides, and Dunn finally had to ask: "Do you mind if we turn around at the next crossroads?"

"Not at all," replied Spruance, smiling to himself, for he knew the next crossroads were five miles away.

At sea Spruance would often pace the deck of his cabin, engrossed in thought; or stare fixedly at a large chart of the Pacific, dismissing interruptions with a wave of his hand while his mind probed and evaluated every phase of a battle plan. Once the tactics and strategy of an operation were decided upon, he would issue a general order to his subordinate commanders, in whom he was wont to place the "utmost confidence." It was their assigned task to work out the details of an operation and he rarely interfered with their judgments. When he did, it was usually because someone down the line had fumbled his job. In brief, then, this was the man to whom Nimitz entrusted the command of Task Force Sixteen. He was not an aviator, he had never commanded a carrier force before, and he was virtually without battle experience, but Spruance was to prove that leadership is not made in battle; it is only exhibited.[5]

Had the coming battle belonged to an earlier time, Nimitz would have gone to sea with his fleet, but these titanic movements of forces—Yamamoto's and his own—obliged him to remain at a central position, from where he could command Midway's air power, Theobald's cruisers, and his three vulnerable aircraft carriers at one and the same time. During the last week of May he transmitted his Operational Plan 29–42 to the fleet. In it he enumerated what he believed was the strength of Japanese forces and stated that he expected Yamamoto to make a spirited attack on Midway, that the American task forces would be hunted resolutely by enemy reconnaissance aircraft and submarines and that the *Yorktown, Enterprise* and *Hornet* would be the first order of business for Japanese carrier planes. Fletcher and Spruance were instructed to strike at the enemy, governing themselves by "the principle of calculated risk," which required that they expose themselves to superior forces only if there existed a good chance of inflicting greater harm upon the Japanese.

Admiral Nimitz reasoned that the Japanese carriers under Nagumo would approach Midway on a southeasterly or easterly course. This meant that search planes from the atoll, fanning out westward over the sea for a distance of 600 to 700 miles, would eventually discover them. But the enemy might encounter some moderately dirty weather—a likely prospect northwest of Midway—and if this were the case, they could use it as a shield while their bombers came in for the first attack.

Nimitz, of course, was taking a very great risk in putting almost all his resources in the Midway operation. If, through some tragic miscalculation, his own carriers were sighted by the first wave of Japanese bombers, then Fletcher and Spruance, not Midway, would come under a vicious air attack. But risks had to be accepted and Nimitz held to his belief that Nagumo would launch his first flight from a position somewhere northwest of the atoll. To hold a tactical advantage and yet remain unseen, it was necessary for Nimitz to place his carriers on Nagumo's flank, provided, of course, that Nagumo's flank was where Nimitz expected it to be. Accordingly, he ordered Fletcher and Spruance to steam to a position known simply as Point "Luck," which was situated about 350 miles to the northeast of Midway. Here the two carrier commanders were to wait until Yamamoto's ships were sighted by American patrol planes. As soon as the Japanese carriers were seen, Fletcher and Spruance, still undetected (at least, theoretically), could launch a heavy air strike against them, knock them out of the fight and turn their victory march into a shameful retreat.

During the last days of May the atmosphere grew tense around Nimitz's headquarters as the American task forces prepared for battle. Pickup trucks shuttled officers back and forth along the docks; cargo nets bulging with ammunition boxes were swung to the decks of ships; new planes were hoisted on board the *Yorktown*, while the last repairs were being made; young sailors checked the Watch, Quarter and Station Bill to make sure they knew where they were supposed to be when the battle started. Chief engineers checked over their spare parts; pilots looked over their planes; navigators thumbed through their chart portfolios; and the rest, stealing a few minutes from the swift pace, went ashore for a couple of drinks and farewells.

Almost 3500 miles to the westward, Japanese naval officers were toasting the Emperor with tiny cups of rice wine, for

their time had come too. They had a boundless faith in Yamamoto, whom they venerated almost as a god. They would
move out with him, their colors nailed to the mast, unyield-
ing, invincible. Only a very few were skeptical, and none, as
far as can be known, envisaged failure.

The first units of Yamamoto's armada to get underway were
the submarines. Two minelaying submersibles, under the
command of Commander Yasuo Fujimori, left very early to
deliver aviation gasoline and lubricating oil to French Frigate
Shoals, a coral cluster lying about 450 miles westnorthwest of
Oahu. This cargo was earmarked for some Kawanishi flying
boats which were supposed to fly scouting missions over the
area before the battle began. But Fujimori did not find the
planes in the appointed place; instead he sighted through his
periscope several United States seaplanes and a tender swinging at anchor. Since French Frigate Shoals was in American
hands and his own aircraft did not appear, he quit the area
and returned to Japan.[6]

The rest of the submarines, which were to reconnoiter the
waters around Oahu, also left much earlier than Yamamoto's
surface forces, and after poking about Pearl Harbor for a
while they spread themselves out on their prearranged patrol
lines, arriving on station on 3 June. If this operational time-
table was inspired by Yamamoto's strong belief that Nimitz
would do nothing until Midway had fallen, then their arrival
on the patrol line could not, from the Japanese point of view,
have been considered too late. Admiral Nimitz, however, who
was by no means conforming to Yamamoto's expectations,
had his task forces far to the west of the patrol line when the
enemy submarines finally took up their stations, and thus they

missed a golden opportunity to intercept the American carriers, or at least report their presence at sea to Admiral Nagumo.

It hardly seems possible that Yamamoto, would have cut the corners so fine, even if he did expect Nimitz to react slowly. The submarines were of vital importance in the first stages of the battle and their failure to get into proper position early enough was to cost the Japanese heavily.[7] One piece of postwar criticism of the patrol, coming from Captain Y. Watanabe of Yamamoto's staff, blamed the poor deployment of the submarines for the Midway disaster,[8] yet Admiral Spruance slammed right across the hypothetical line on 30 May before any Japanese submarines reached it, and Admiral Fletcher, riding in higher latitudes, later brushed its northern terminus. It can only be concluded that the location of the patrol line was reasonably right, its time of activation seriously wrong.

While the submarines were leisurely taking up their stations, Yamamoto's surface units were getting up steam. The first group to weigh anchor was Rear Admiral Kakuta's Second Carrier Striking Force, which was assigned to the Aleutian phase of the operation. On 25 May he led his two carriers, *Ryujo* and *Junyo,* and their supporting cruisers and destroyers out of the harbor of Ominato, which rests at the extreme northern end of the main island of Honshu. By evening he had his ships through the Tsugaru Strait separating Honshu from Hokkaido and was already pushing into the deep water of the northern Pacific. Two days later Kakuta was followed to sea by Vice Admiral Moshiro Hosogaya, who was in command of the Aleutians Operation and who brought

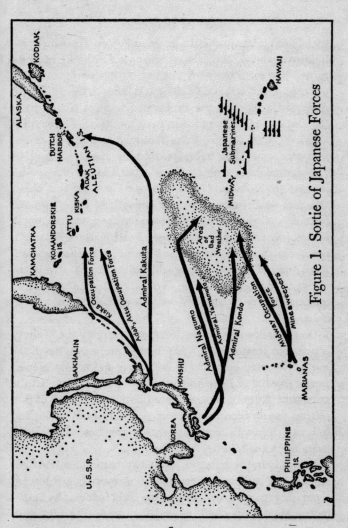

Figure 1. Sortie of Japanese Forces

with him the Attu and Kiska Invasion Forces. The Attu Force followed generally in Kakuta's wake, while the Kiska Force turned to a more northerly heading, later altering course to the eastward. On the 26th, about 600 miles to the southwest, Admiral Nagumo left the insular anchorage of Hiroshima in the Inland Sea. Flying his flag from the *Akagi*, Nagumo led his First Carrier Striking Force through the Bungo Strait and into open water. This force, spearheading the attack, with its four formidable carriers—*Akagi* (Red Castle), *Kaga* (Increased Joy), *Hiryu* (Flying Dragon) and *Soryu* (Green Dragon)—and its combined air strength of more than 260 fighters, dive bombers and torpedo planes, was to smash Midway as it had earlier smashed Pearl Harbor. Second in command of these carriers was former Princeton student Rear Admiral Tamon Yamaguchi, riding confidently in the *Hiryu*, from whose bridge he watched the force's battleships, cruisers, destroyers and tankers take up their cruising positions.

On the following day the transports carrying the Midway occupation troops left their anchorage at Saipan, far to the south, protected by a ring of destroyers and a light cruiser, *Jintsu*, flagship of Rear Admiral Raizo Tanaka. At about the same time, Kurita's Support Group, assigned the task of protecting the invasion convoy, left its moorings at Guam and followed Tanaka's northeasterly course toward Midway, bringing to sea four heavy cruisers.

Vice Admiral Nobutake Kondo's two battleships, one light carrier, five cruisers and escorting destroyers began leaving the anchorage at Hashirajima on the 28th, followed by Yamamoto's Main Force, built around the massive *Yamato*, with two other battleships, a light carrier, one cruiser, two sea-plane carriers and a destroyer screen. The fleet advanced sol-emnly, according to Yamamoto's yeoman, "scattering pearl white waves before it . . . and we were all singing war songs at the top of our lungs."

Thus by 29 May the great Japanese sea march was under-way, and the odds were stacked heavily against the American fleet.

CHAPTER
4

~~~~~~~~

THE FIRST SKIRMISH

*But the time of preparation will pass;
some day the time of action will come.
Can an admiral then sit down and re-
enforce his intellectual grasp of the problem before him by a study of history,
which is simply a study of past experience? Not so; the time of action is upon
him, and he must trust to his horse sense.*
ALFRED THAYER MAHAN

WITH THE IMPENDING battle just over the horizon, Rear Admiral Robert H. English, commander of the submarines attached to the Pacific Fleet, was obliged to make the best possible use of his boats to support Fletcher and Spruance. His
primary task was to sink enemy ships, preferably carriers
and transports, before they got near Midway, and to do this
he divided his available submarine strength into three groups.
Poring over a chart of the Pacific, English marked off the
areas he wanted patrolled. The first area, reduced to funda-
mentals, was in the shape of a fan, with its handle covering

Midway, its left edge pointing westsouthwest, and the right edge running in a northerly direction. Eleven submarines [1] were positioned along this wide patrol arc, shielding Midway at distances varying from 60 to 210 miles. A second group of three boats [2] was assigned to a scouting line over 400 miles to the eastnortheast of the atoll, in case some Japanese ships slipped by and headed for Oahu, while a third group of four submarines [3] was stationed 300 miles due north of Oahu. Finally a lone sentinel, the slow-moving *Cuttlefish,* rode out to a position about 650 miles to the west of Midway. The rest were sent on patrol to the Aleutians. [4]

When Admiral English composed his strategical deployment, some submarines were at dockside in Pearl Harbor, the rest were either on their way to or had already arrived at their routine patrol stations. Immediately there was a grand reshuffling of operational orders. A tense atmosphere hung over Midway, where some boats put in for fuel before going out on their new war patrol. A hasty conference was held in the cramped wardroom of the *Flying Fish,* where a Marine officer said: "If you can sink two of their carriers, we'll beat them off. . . ." [5]

Submarines departed into the vast wastes of the western Pacific. More came to Midway, fueled, and then glided away to their assigned stations, and before Nagumo's carriers were within striking distance the atoll had an advance guard far out at sea.

Meanwhile, the American surface fleet was moving out. On 28 May Admiral Spruance stood on the flag bridge of the *Enterprise,* watching Task Force Sixteen sortie for battle. His flagship was the seventh naval vessel to bear the famous

name. At the same time the *Hornet* got underway, under the
command of Capain Marc A. Mitscher. While at Pearl Harbor
her planes, as a usual procedure, had been taken ashore,
but there had not been time to hoist them back on board
before sailing. Consequently the entire Air Group had to fly
out to sea and land on the *Hornet*. One dive bomber developed engine trouble and her pilot, Lieutenant W. J. Wid-
helm, unable to get his craft off the runway, was flown to his
ship in the rear seat of a torpedo plane.[6]

The combined air strength under Spruance's command
amounted to fifty-four fighters, seventy-five dive bombers and
twenty-nine torpedo planes—no match for Nagumo's superior
strength, but the *Yorktown's* aircraft, soon to join Task Force
Sixteen, and the planes from Midway were to alter the odds of
battle. In support of the *Enterprise* and *Hornet* were the
cruisers under Rear Admiral Thomas C. Kinkaid, including
the heavy *New Orleans, Minneapolis, Vincennes, Northamp-
ton* and *Pensacola,* and the light *Atlanta;* and farther out were
the nine hard-driving destroyers of Squadrons One and Six.[7]
And, finally, came the tankers *Cimarron* and *Platte,* each with
a screening destroyer.

After pushing through Kauai Channel, Task Force Sixteen
set a base course of 296° and headed for Point "Luck."

On 29 May the drydock which had cradled the *Yorktown*
was flooded and the ship was warped into deep water. That
evening Admiral Fletcher looked over his charts once more
and reexamined the intelligence reports that had been ac-
cumulating. Finally he retired but was up early the next
morning. At 9 o'clock, with a warm Hawaiian sun already

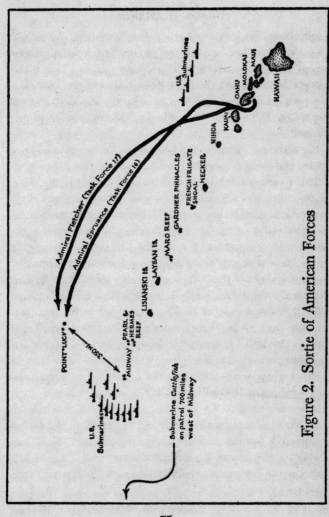

Figure 2. Sortie of American Forces

high above the horizon, Task Force Seventeen put to sea, her air strength consisting of twenty-five fighters, thirty-seven bombers and thirteen torpedo planes. The heavy cruiser *Portland* and the light cruiser *Astoria* gave her close support, while the screen was held by the five destroyers of Squadron Two—*Hammann, Hughes, Morris, Anderson* and *Russell*.

By this time Spruance had been at sea for two days and was many hundreds of miles to the northwest of Oahu. Everyone felt the ominous tension which mounts before battle. Most of the officers, of necessity, knew where they were going; the enlisted men, until they were told, had to depend on "scuttle-butt," prophecies in the chow line, or the spontaneous and often wild conjectures of would-be strategists. But most of them knew that something decisive was about to happen.

On the night of the 30th, some twelve hours after Admiral Fletcher's ships had bucked through the Kauai Channel, Nimitz radioed another intelligence report to his task-force commanders, giving them a more accurate estimate of Yamamoto's strength.[8] It was not reassuring, but if Fletcher and Spruance managed to reach their striking position without detection, they would still have the advantage of surprise on their side. On the following day Spruance made a slight change of course to the left and ordered his ships to take on fuel from the tankers *Cimarron* and *Platte*. With the fueling completed, Spruance resumed course for Point "Luck," arriving on the first of June. At the same time, Captain Mitscher wrote out a message to be read over the *Hornet's* loudspeaker system:

"The enemy are approaching for an attempt to seize Midway," it said. "This attack will probably be accompanied by a feint at western Alaska. We are going to prevent them from taking Midway, if possible. Be ready and keep on the alert. Let's get a few more yellowtails." [9] There was no longer any doubt about the task force's mission.

Meanwhile Fletcher, who had been bending on knots to close the gap which separated him from Spruance, also reached his fueling rendezvous. Once more Captain Ralph Henkle of the *Platte* and Commander Russell Ihrig of the *Cimarron* ordered the cradles swung out, and Task Force Seventeen filled up its tanks. Fletcher then pushed on for Point "Luck," while Spruance, who was already there, came about on a reciprocal course in search of him. In the afternoon of June 2nd, Spruance sighted the *Yorktown* in a position about 350 miles to the northeast of Midway. Soon after, Admiral Fletcher assumed tactical command of both forces, keeping them separated but within visual signalling distance of each other. On this same day Admiral Spruance sent a message to all the ships under his immediate command. It read in part:

AN ATTACK FOR THE PURPOSE OF CAPTURING MIDWAY IS EXPECTED. THE ATTACKING FORCE MAY BE COMPOSED OF ALL COMBATANT TYPES INCLUDING FOUR OR FIVE CARRIERS, TRANSPORTS AND TRAIN VESSELS. IF PRESENCE OF TASK FORCE 16 AND 17 REMAINS UNKOWN TO ENEMY WE SHOULD BE ABLE TO MAKE SURPRISE FLANK ATTACKS ON ENEMY CARRIERS FROM POSITION NORTHEAST OF MIDWAY. FURTHER OPERATIONS WILL BE BASED ON RESULT OF THESE ATTACKS, DAMAGE INFLICTED BY MIDWAY FORCES, AND INFORMATION OF ENEMY MOVEMENTS. THE SUC-

CESSFUL CONCLUSION OF THE OPERATION NOW COMMENCING
WILL BE OF GREAT VALUE TO OUR COUNTRY.

Captain Elliott Buckmaster also informed his crew what
the *Yorktown* was heading for, and he promised them shore
leave as soon as the battle was won. For most of the officers
and men, the promise of a breathing spell was the most welcome news of all. Since the ship had left on her last war
cruise, she had been at sea continuously for nearly three and
a half months. As a result, her stores were very low and her
cooks, finally scraping the bottom of the larder, were forced
to serve up a monotonous fare of tinned meats and dehy-
drated eggs and potatoes. Everyone on board recalled the
day when the last steak was placed on a tray and paraded
about the flight deck, along with a big sign which read:

SPECIAL SIDE SHOW

Big T-Bone Steak

The Only One in Captivity

10¢ a peek

Do not touch

The two task forces cruised in the vicinity of Point "Luck,"
waiting for the message which would tell them that an
American submarine or patrol plane had discovered Nagumo's carriers. Fighter planes on combat air patrol guarded
the vulnerable carriers below. However, neither Fletcher
nor Spruance wanted to be caught by a sudden Japanese air
attack and therefore, at different times during their long vigil,

they sent off reconnaissance flights to the northwest. The planes found nothing on the broad stretch of sea, and foul weather forced some to return.

Slowly the sun set, night came on like cerulean smoke, and each ship went through the accustomed changing of the watch. The next morning a resolute Admiral Fletcher read despatches and patiently waited for the Japanese to show themselves. Spruance paced the deck of his cabin, thinking with the concentration of a chess player. And so the third day of the lovely month of June began.

By now Admiral Hosogaya's Aleutians Occupation Force was driving in two prongs toward the mist-shrouded islands of the Alaskan chain. He was supported by Admiral Kakuta's Second Carrier Force, which had been steaming on an easterly course but was now northbound, heading for Dutch Harbor. Admiral Kondo, after leaving Japan on 27 May, steamed on an eastsoutheasterly heading, while the Midway Invasion Force under Admirals Kurita and Tanaka, having departed from Guam at the same time, was on an eastnortheasterly course. On 3 June these forces were already joined, with Kondo's ships protecting the exultant Japanese troops riding in the transports. Their course was approximately 080°, directly on a line with Midway. Nagumo's four carriers, after reaching a point about 900 miles to the northwest of Midway, swung around to a course of 130° and headed on a straight line for the atoll. About 300 miles behind them was Yamamoto's Main Force, bringing up the rear. Yamamoto seemed at the moment destined for immortality. His titanic forces were closing in on Midway from the northwest and southwest, while Kakuta, feinting to the north, was expected to trick Nimitz into dividing his feeble strength.

Even the weather, so often a decisive factor in the evolution of battle, was working in favor of the Japanese.[10] The aerological conditions Yamamoto needed for his operation were threefold. During the approach squally weather and low clouds were necessary to conceal his movements from American scout planes. When ready for the "softening up" phase of the operation, he needed a favorable wind, both in direction and velocity, so that Nagumo could launch and recover his aircraft without making excessive advances and withdrawals to and from the target area, and at the same time he needed clear skies and good visibility over Midway. For the actual invasion of the atoll he wanted continued good visibility over the target so that his aircraft might quickly gain command of the air, but this had to be coupled with light breezes, thus assuring a quiet sea for the amphibious landings. Yamamoto got almost exactly what he had prayed for.

At this time of the year the Pacific storm pattern usually leads to turbulences northwest of Midway, which move eastward, bringing clouds and rain. As this broad band of morbid weather rolls eastward, it tends to break up into ragged cloud formations and sporadic squalls, and by the time it reaches the vicinity of Midway it is usually dissipated.

In the first days of June a stationary high pressure area, located to the northeast of Midway, was causing other fronts, especially to the west and northwest, to decelerate; and to the south of the atoll all that remained of the frontal system formerly centered there were cloud fragments which limited but did not eliminate visibility. But early in the morning of

3 June a weak storm area began to develop about 700 miles to the northwest of Midway, and from its center a front of cool air spread out to the south and southwest. As this air mass moved toward the northeast, it ran into a warm front situated about 200 miles west of Midway. Soon the whole area to the northwest was overcast with low, gray clouds and intermittent rain, and a gentle wind blew out of the southwest, where visibility was often reduced to two miles. This offered Nagumo's pilots very poor flying conditions, but since he was still far from his launching position, the weather, concealing him from scouting aircraft, was actually a blessing in disguise. The troopships approaching Midway from the southwest were not so lucky, since they were just then steaming in a neutral area between the two frontal systems, which was marked by only partial cloudiness and visibility up to twenty miles.

Midway itself was bathed in sunlight, as Yamamoto had hoped it would be, but moving westward from the atoll toward the warm front, the ceiling lowered to 1000 feet and visibility was reduced to a maximum of twelve miles. As long as these conditions prevailed, Midway would be spotlighted under a bright sky while the approaching enemy remained hidden under rain clouds.

The weather hanging over the Aleutian Islands was also dense, concealing the movements of Admiral Kakuta, who was bringing his two carriers, *Ryujo* and *Junyo,* to a launching position about 180 miles south of Unalaska. At the northeastern corner of this island lay his target, the naval base of Dutch Harbor, resting under the massive Makushin Volcano, whose cone climbed skyward to a height of 6,680 feet but was, as usual, shrouded in heavy mists. There is little darkness during the summer in these high latitudes, and the cheerless sun on 3 June rose at a few minutes before 3 o'clock. At the same time Kakuta's planes, loaded with heavy bombs, were leaving the carriers and speeding northward through the damp, diaphanous air. Before they arrived over the target the fog lifted, revealing Dutch Harbor. The first strike, dumping its bombs with vengeance, was soon followed by a second strike. Before the morning was over, Dutch Harbor was strewn with the wreckage of planes and buildings, and about a dozen soldiers and sailors fell. Huge funnels of black smoke spiraled skyward from burning fuel tanks. A few days later Kiska and Attu were in Japanese hands.

In the meantime, scouting planes from Midway had been searching as far westward as their fuel supply and the weather allowed. Toward 9 o'clock in the morning of the 3rd, Ensign Jewell H. Reid, piloting a Catalina, was flying through clouds about 700 miles to the west of the atoll. Suddenly a pocket opened up in the overcast, revealing the presence of a large fleet of ships driving eastward. Reid had found the Midway Occupation Force. After tracking it for a time to determine its approximate course and speed, he slammed a contact report to Midway. Commander Cyril T. Simard, commanding the atoll's air strength, ordered a flight of Army B-17 bombers to intercept the ships, which were thought to be Yamamoto's main force. In the afternoon, flying at about 1000 feet, the bombers sighted the transports trailing their feathery wakes. A high-level attack began; bombs whistled down and smashed into the sea, leaving white blobs of water amid the ships, which were now making frantic turns to the left and right. Then the surrounding sky erupted with puffs of antiaircraft fire as the supporting ships raised their guns to the bombers. At the end of the attack the Army bombardiers were sure they had scored damaging hits on two large battleships or cruisers and two auxiliary vessels. Actually, the "hits" were near misses. However, Admiral English had to assume that the pilots' reports were reasonably accurate, and so ordered Lieutenant Commander M. P. Hottel, skipper of the *Cuttlefish*, to hunt down the crippled "battleships" which, of course, were never found. During the moonlit evening of 3–4 June the Japanese transports came under another attack, this time from torpedo planes, but the Navy fliers who made this assault managed to hit only the tanker *Akebono Maru*, which shook off the blow and eventually crept back to her position in the Midway Occupation Force. The first skirmishes of the battle had begun.

The contact report indicating erroneously that it was the Main Force which had been sighted was also received by the flagship of Task Force Seventeen. Admiral Fletcher would have had to revise his tactical plans immediately if the report were accurate, but the bearing of the enemy force was given as 261° from Midway and this threw doubt on the force's reported composition. Fletcher had made a meticulous analysis of all previous intelligence reports on the movement of Japanese forces, which foretold that the main thrust would come from the northwest where the weather was foul, not from the more westerly direction given in the contact report. Since he had to maintain radio silence so that the enemy would not know of his presence, Fletcher could not ask the pilot for an amplifying message and was thus left to his own judgment.

At this point the first important command decision of the battle was made, for Fletcher concluded that the ships sighted by Reid were part of the enemy's invasion fleet, while the first air strike against Midway would come out of the northwestern sky at dawn of the next day. That evening he swung around to the southwest in order to station his three carriers at a favorable launching position on Nagumo's flank. Thus he and Spruance would be ready to pounce on the Japanese admiral as soon as his own carriers broke through the fringe of squalls which had been shielding them. The rendezvous position for the early morning of 4 June was 31° 30' North, 176° 30' West, which would place the American task forces about 200 miles north and slightly to the east of Midway Island.[11]

Fletcher's lookouts, continuously scanning broad sectors of the sky, found no hostile search planes buzzing about; nor had his destroyers made a sonar contact on an enemy submarine. As evening came on, Fletcher was able to conclude that the Japanese carrier admiral was pushing toward Midway, ignorant of the fact that three American carriers were waiting for him—that, in fact, the hunter had become the hunted.

During the tense night of 3–4 June, Nagumo drove hard through a blanket of fog on a southeasterly course toward the atoll, while Fletcher steamed on a southwesterly heading. The imaginary projection of their course lines formed a "V," the point of which was located somewhere to the northwest of Midway.

Nagumo had lost some of the aggressive spirit of a successful fleet commander, for he had had sufficient time to reflect upon the weaknesses of his command. During the training period which preceded the Midway undertaking, he had witnessed the excessively poor results obtained by some of his pilots during several mock torpedo attacks carried out in May; other pilots, because of the demands of basic training, had not had enough practice at dive bombing; and Nagumo felt that almost none, save a handful of the older fliers, had had sufficient opportunity to practice carrier landings. There had been time to teach the pilots only the barest essentials.

Later on, after the Midway disaster soured him, Nagumo was to write bitterly:

"Because of the need for replacements and transfers of personnel, the combat efficiency of each ship had been greatly lowered . . . Training in group formations could not be satisfactorily conducted because of the limitation in time . . . Added to this, we had practically no intelligence concerning the enemy. We never knew to the end where or how many enemy carriers there were . . . we participated in this operation with meager training and without knowledge of the enemy." [12]

No matter how justified Nagumo's hindsighted complaints might have been, Commander Mitsuo Fuchida, *Akagi's* air officer, felt that Nagumo had lost his original vigor as a naval leader. Fuchida, who succumbed to a sudden seizure of appendicitis and thus did not lead the Midway attack as he had led the one on Pearl Harbor, had first met Nagumo in 1933 and soon learned to respect him with "awe and admiration." They met again in 1941, when Fuchida was sent to the

Akagi for flying duty. His earlier esteem for Nagumo soon underwent some painful changes, for he writes:

". . . Nagumo had changed, and I began to feel dissatisfied with his apparent conservatism and passiveness . . . he was as warmhearted and sympathetic as ever, but his once-vigorous fighting spirit seemed to be gone, and with it his stature as an outstanding naval leader. Instead he seemed rather average, and I was suddenly aware of his increased age." [13]

Even if this rather unhappy appraisal of Nagumo is a correct one, it should not be left without briefly noting that Yamamoto himself was also to blame for the enormous disaster which overwhelmed his Midway ambitions. It is clear that he deprived Nagumo of valuable antiaircraft fire power by holding back his own powerful ships, hundreds of miles astern of the Japanese carriers; but an even more serious error was his apparent confidence that Admiral Nimitz, floundering about at his Pearl Harbor headquarters, was unaware of Japanese plans.

Be that as it may, there were immediate problems for Nagumo to brood over during the dark hours of 3–4 June. He was still under a blanket of low hanging clouds and the wind was light, a fact which would complicate the launching and landing of aircraft. During the small hours of the 4th the weather began to clear somewhat as the Japanese carriers broke through the frontal fringe. There were occasional showers along the cold front, but a bright star could be seen now and then through the scattered clouds which drifted between 1000 and 2500 feet above the dark sea. There was a moderate northwesterly wind blowing, but this began to veer about to the southeast and soon visibility opened up from almost nothing to a maximum of sixteen miles,[14] a fact which raised Nagumo's spirits. Except for the feeble wind, conditions had become almost ideal for him; the increased visibility would enable him to launch his planes for the Midway strike, while the low, broken cloud cover and scattered showers would hide him from enemy scout planes. Or so he thought.

Far to the east, the American ships followed a zigzag plan over a smooth sea. Overhead a blanket of cumulus clouds rode on the crest of a weak warm front, blotting out the stars. Everyone waited for the dawn. Some 200 miles to the south Midway's defenders were aroused from exhausted sleep at 3 o'clock in the morning. Submarines, friend and foe alike, were prowling across the ocean; and back at Pearl Harbor lights were burning in the operations room of the Commander-in-Chief, Pacific Fleet.

At about 4 o'clock that morning eleven Navy Catalina patrol planes were readied for take-off at Midway. Fifteen minutes later they roared off into the western darkness, while the first faint light of the rising sun washed the sky at their backs. At the same time enemy planes were warming up on the flight decks of Nagumo's Striking Force. At 4:30 the Japanese admiral gave the command to launch planes. Air officers aboard the four Japanese carriers began swinging green take-off lanterns. Then the first Zero fighters shot down the runways, lifted gracefully into the wind, and orbited above the fleet until the rest of the flight joined up. Next came the bombers, loaded with 550-pound missiles, and before dawn broke at a few minutes to 5 o'clock there were 108 Japanese planes in the air, formed into "V's." Except for rents in the overcast, the fliers would have cloud cover most of the way in, and by the time they arrived over the atoll it would be clear daylight.

As the Japanese pilots sped along, led by *Hiryu's* air commander, Lieutenant Joichi Tomonaga, Nagumo and those left with him could only look at the sea and wait. Nagumo's flagship, *Akagi*, was out in front of the right column of the Striking Force, with the *Kaga* trailing astern by about two miles. About the same distance away on *Akagi's* port side was the *Hiryu*, with Captain Tameo Kaku in command. Two miles astern of Kaku rode the *Hiryu's* sister ship, *Soryu*. Her skipper was Captain Ryusaku Yanagimoto. For all of them, now, the Midway strike was underway.

Admiral Fletcher waited, somewhat anxiously, for some word about Japanese ship movements, especially the carriers, which he had to cripple swiftly. He could not risk a Pyrrhic victory by getting himself sunk too. The silent darkness and the imminence of battle added to his anxiety: his own flank might be threatened at the very moment he thought he was threatening the Japanese admiral's. So at 4:30, almost at the same time the enemy planes were leaving their carriers, Fletcher, to prevent a surprise attack by Japanese planes, sent ten Dauntless scout planes to sweep over the sea area to the north of his own forces.[15] They flew out, fanwise, into the cool, cloudy darkness for a hundred miles or more, some of them spearing into the cold front which Nagumo was just then breaking through. During their outbound flight the sun rose, giving them an occasional glimpse of the water below, but the Japanese carriers were farther to the south and none of the *Yorktown's* pilots was given the dramatic chance of radioing their location, course and speed to Admiral Fletcher.

In the meantime the Navy Catalinas which left Midway at 4:30 were patrolling to the west through dark, billowy clouds touched by the first flush of dawn. Flying toward them were Nagumo's fighters and bombers, speeding over a brightening sea. By 5 o'clock the sun had risen above the rim of the eastern horizon. Castled clouds covered the area and searching pilots from both the *Yorktown* and Midway Atoll found it difficult to get a good glimpse of the sea below.

After reaching the end of their search, the *Yorktown's* pilots began their return flight; Midway's PBY's, pushing through the cloud masses, continued on patrol. The sky was quite bright now, but to the west a gloomy overcast poured down cold rain.

About 5:30 the pilots of Catalina Flight 58, Lieutenants Howard Ady and William Chase, soared over a deep abyss in the cloud blanket and saw below them the morning sea. Suddenly they spied the white feather of a ship's wake to the north. Nosing over for a better look, they found a second wake, then more. The light was quite good now and in a few minutes they recognized the uncluttered decks of Japanese aircraft carriers. Immediately they radioed Midway:

ENEMY CARRIERS.

The American forces, tuned to Midway's radio frequency, intercepted the message at 5:34. Automatically a stream of questions ran through Fletcher's mind. How many carriers?

Where were they? What was their course and speed? Were
their decks empty, or were aircraft on board, warming up
for a strike? He had to wait for the answers, for a lookout on
board the heavy cruiser *Tone*, part of Nagumo's support
group, had sighted the American plane and batteries of antiaircraft guns opened fire. While the PBY, wings aslant,
ducked into the clouds, several Zeros began climbing in a
desperate effort to shoot the plane down. But the clouds
which had been shielding the Japanese Striking Force now
saved the PBY. The plane winged over toward the east,
found another hole in the cloud mass, and a few minutes
later glided through it for another look around. Below was a
broad formation of enemy planes streaking eastward toward
the sun. Immediately another contact report was hammered
out to Midway:

FROM FLIGHT 58. MANY PLANES HEADING MIDWAY, BEARING
320°, DISTANCE 150.

And a few minutes later Flight 92 radioed:

TWO CARRIERS AND BATTLESHIPS BEARING 320°, DISTANCE
180, COURSE 135, SPEED 25.[16]

Fletcher's staff officers got busy drafting lines on a large
chart of the western Pacific—one on a reciprocal bearing of
315°, leading away from Midway, another leading away
from the *Yorktown's* known position to the reported where-
abouts of the Japanese carriers. At the time of these contact
reports Admiral Fletcher, who still had his dawn patrol in

the air, was about ten miles to the northeast of Task Force Sixteen.[17] He had to take immediate action, but since he first had to recover his search planes, he sent a message to Admiral Spruance at 6:07. "Proceed southwesterly," it read, "and attack enemy carriers when definitely located." Fletcher stated that he would follow Spruance as soon as he had gathered in his reconnaissance aircraft.

This was the word Spruance had been waiting for. He ordered his fleet on an attack course while the General Quarters alarm clanged throughout the ships of Task Force Sixteen. According to his plot, Spruance was less than 200 miles away from the enemy carriers and he sped southwestward at 25 knots to get within good striking distance before he was discovered. The sea was smooth, with occasional mild gusts of wind ruffling the surface. Above were cumulus clouds, and just below their base the air was clear. At an altitude of 1500 feet one could see for fifty miles around. It was a perfect day for carrier warfare.

Captain George D. Murray, *Enterprise's* commanding officer, had already worked out the order of launching with his Air Group Commander, Lieutenant Commander Clarence W. McClusky. Thirty-three bombers were to head for Nagumo's carriers, fifteen of them with a 1000-pound bomb each, twelve with a 500-pounder plus two small 100-pound bombs, and six with one 500-pounder apiece—fifty-seven bombs in all. This bombing force was to be divided into two waves, one to be led by Lieutenant Richard H. Best, the other by Lieutenant Wilmer E. Gallaher. A second force of fourteen torpedo planes was to be commanded by Lieutenant Commander Eugene E. Lindsey, and the fighter screen was under the command of Lieutenant James S. Gray with ten aircraft. Thirty-six fighters were kept out of the attack, eighteen to patrol over the task force, the other eighteen to relieve them.

At the same time, planes were being spotted on the *Hornet's* flight deck: thirty-five bombers to be led in two groups by Lieutenant Commanders Robert R. Johnson and Walter F. Rodee; fifteen torpedo planes under the command of Lieutenant Commander John C. Waldron; and, finally, a division of ten fighters, Lieutenant Commander Samuel G. Mitchell commanding.

The fliers were waiting in the readyroom for a final briefing. They were tense and tired, for they had already been given two false starts within the last five hours. A vague heedlessness had hold of them and they grumbled about the delay. But Admiral Spruance, wanting to get within one hundred miles of his target, held to his course so that his pilots would have plenty of fuel to return to their carriers once the attack was launched. Taking into account the converging courses of Nagumo's force and his own, he estimated that he would reach a favorable launching position at about 9 o'clock. Captain Miles Browning, who had been Admiral Halsey's chief of staff and was thus accustomed to spontaneous and vigorous action, pressed for an earlier strike. Browning felt that the time to catch the Japanese admiral was when his carriers were loaded with refueling aircraft, and so he urged Spruance to launch his own strike two hours earlier.

Admiral Spruance, of course, understood the necessity of hitting the enemy carriers when they were unable to retaliate, but he knew that launching his planes at 7 o'clock would mean that most of them would have barely enough fuel to return to their roost—some perhaps not enough, forcing the unlucky pilots into the sea. Yet, if he waited too long a Japanese scout plane might find him and then he would be no better off than Nagumo, who was under the illusion that he had not yet been discovered. The demands of war are relentless and Spruance had to obey them; but he could console himself with the fact that each plane carried an inflatable life raft, and if he succeeded in smashing the Japanese carriers, then he could send destroyers ahead on a scouting line to pick up the downed fliers. He agreed to an early launch, and subsequent events proved the wisdom of his decision.

Those were the events, unforeseen in Yamamoto's battle plans, now closing in on Nagumo. While Tomonaga was leading his planes toward Midway, Nagumo ordered an extensive air reconnaissance of the sea to the north, east and south, with Midway lying within the search arc. One plane left the *Akagi* and flew south for 300 miles, made a dogleg to the left for about half an hour, and then headed back to the carrier, while another aircraft from the *Kaga* flew a similar pattern to the southsoutheast. The rest of the scouting aircraft were seaplanes; one from the battleship *Haruna*, which was to make a short 150-mile sweep to the northnortheast; two from the cruiser *Chikuma*, which fanned out to the northeast just as the Midway attackers were forming up; and two more from the cruiser *Tone*. It was with one of the *Tone's* search planes that Nagumo's star began to fall.

Tone's Number Three plane got off at 4:42 with no trouble

and headed out on a southeasterly course, thus missing Fletcher and Spruance by a wide margin. Plane Number Four, however, whose wedge-shaped pattern almost enclosed the American ships within its search limits, ran into some difficulties. Scheduled to depart at about 4:30, the aircraft did not leave the cruiser until 5 o'clock because a faulty catapult on the *Tone's* stern delayed its take-off. It was this lone aircraft, launched late, which eventually sighted and reported the American ships.

CHAPTER
5

~~~~~~~~

NAGUMO'S ORDEAL

*Now the heavy hand of war dealt equal
woe and counterchange of death; in even
balance conquerors and conquered slew
and fell; nor one nor other knows of retreat.*   VIRGIL: *Aeneid*

UP TO THE time the Midway search planes took off at 4:30
on 4 June, the only Japanese ships Midway was aware of
were Tanaka's invasion transports and their supporting vessels moving up from the westsouthwest at a lazy speed of
about 10 knots. So immediately after the PBY's shoved off
to look for Nagumo, Flight 92, consisting of sixteen Army
B-17's (the famed and rugged Flying Fortresses) roared off
into the western gloom to strike at Tanaka's troopships. Almost exactly one hour after the last Flying Fortress lifted its
wheels off the runway, the searching PBY found Tomonaga's
bomb-laden planes and that electrifying message from the
PBY crackled in Midway's radio receivers:

MANY PLANES HEADING MIDWAY . . .

Instantly the remaining planes were ordered to clear the field. As they were taking off, Midway's radar operators were picking up a fast-moving target to the northwest. At 5:50 they reported the presence of many planes, 93 miles from Midway. Within minutes this radar contact was followed by another aircraft sighting of two carriers and many other ships on a course of 135°, speed 25 knots. At this moment the air-raid sirens began, wailing above the roar of the last plane to leave the field. It was now 6 o'clock and every aircraft that could fly was in the air. At the same time Lieutenant Colonel Walter C. Sweeney, leading his flight of B-17's toward the transports, was ordered to wing northward and attack the Japanese carriers, since the troopships obviously had become secondary targets.

One flight of thirteen Marine fighter planes, most of them obsolete, was under the command of Major Floyd B. Parks, driving hard toward Tomonaga's incoming aircraft. Another equally small group of Marine fighters, led by Major Kirk Armistead, had been sent more to the westward to be in a favorable position in case another attack wave stabbed at Midway from that direction. But as soon as Parks spotted the Japanese planes, at about 6:15, Armistead was ordered to join him. These twenty-six Marine aircraft, twenty of which were of the stubby, slow "Buffalo" type and had seen better days, were about to match themselves against Tomonaga's escort of thirty-six fast and highly maneuverable Zero fighters.[1]

Bypassing the Japanese air strike were two other units of Marine planes, heading far out to sea toward the enemy carriers. The first group, made up of sixteen dive bombers led by Major Lofton R. Henderson, were of the same type which were at about this time being spotted on the flight decks of the *Enterprise* and *Hornet*. The other unit, commanded by Major Benjamin W. Norris, was composed of eleven "Vindicator" bombers, which the Marines contemptuously called "vibrators." They were, like the "Buffalos," built for a different kind of war, and their elongated plexiglas canopies made them resemble winged greenhouses. Yet Norris's planes might have gotten some hits, Henderson's even more, had these heroic bombing squadrons been covered by fighters. The pilot of a level- or dive-bombing aircraft cannot fight off enemy interceptors and aim a bomb at the same time, but there were unfortunately no fighters to spare.

The same lack of support beset the six Navy "Avenger" torpedo planes, which were also heading for the carriers, under the command of Lieutenant Langdon K. Feiberling, as were the Army's four B-26's, led by Captain James F. Collins. To make a torpedo attack, such a plane must come in low, flying through intense antiaircraft fire, and steady on an attack course from which there can be no flinching until the pilot reaches the torpedo release point. As the approach is made, the pilot must rely heavily on his own fighters to keep the enemy's interceptors off his tail, praying all the while that the shipboard gunners firing at him are poor marksmen. So the various flights which took off from Midway on that morning of 4 June were doomed, with the exception of Colonel Sweeney's Flying Fortresses, which were fairly well protected with their own guns, were remarkably durable, and did their bombing from great altitudes.

Since Major Parks had been vectored out from Midway to intercept the Japanese planes, it was he who struck the first blow, but with only twelve aircraft since one of his planes developed engine trouble and had to leave the flight. When Tomonaga was still about fifteen to twenty minutes away from his objective, Parks saw him flying in a tight "V" formation about two miles above the surface of the sea, his seventy-two bombers and thirty-six fighters winging toward the atoll like a disciplined flight of wild geese. Captain J. F. Carey, fortunate enough to be flying one of the new "Wildcat" fighters, shouted a loud and clear "Tally-ho," the signal for attack, and glided over into a tight dive, followed by the rest of the planes in his division. Then Parks pushed over and in a moment all the Marine fighters were full-throttling toward the Japanese formation. There was a moment of surprise, a few seconds of confusion, but the Japanese Zeros, with incredible speed, climbed up to meet the Marines. Since Major Armistead was still some ten or fifteen miles away, desperately trying to get another knot or two from his antiquated aircraft, Major Parks, with his five "Wildcats" and seven "Buffalos," was facing a fight to the death. Even if he had at that moment commanded twelve planes as good as the Zero, the odds would have been three-to-one.

Still he dove into the attack, shouting orders to his pilots, weaving one way and then another, and trying to shake off a whole flock of enemy fighters. Machine guns chattered; tracer bullets speared across the sky; then there was a burst of flame, followed by the convoluting trail of black smoke which marks the final descent of a fallen airman. Some planes burst into brilliant balls of fire as their gasoline tanks ignited; others disintegrated like clay pigeons at a shooting gallery, their wings whirling through ragged clouds and splashing into the sea. A few of them, torn to shreds by the lashing fire of the Zeros, managed to limp away from the melee, only to crumble apart in their devastating retreat. And so the first Marine attack was driven off.

Tomonaga's bombers now had Midway in sight. There were fragments of puffy clouds drifting in the southerly breeze, but the atoll gleamed in the bright morning sun and the coral barrier reef, which closed around Midway's lagoon, was clearly visible. The Japanese pilots were buoyant. Midway could not withstand the shock of this blow which they, with an assortment of bombs, were about to deliver.

Meanwhile, the Marine gunners on the atoll sighted the Japanese air armada. Their fingers pointed to the morning sky as they watched two flaming planes fall into the sea, like spent cinders—part of Major Parks's disintegrating command. They were to see more planes fall, for a few minutes later Major Armistead, listening with frantic concentration to the babble of voices pouring from his radio receiver, finally sighted his foe. The Japanese planes were almost over the island when Armistead glided into his attack. The air battle was brief, as one plane after another spun into a death dive. The rest of the aged aircraft, unable to compete with Tomonaga's agile Zeros, had to pull out of the fight, but most of them fell in flames as enemy fighters chopped at them from all directions. Of the twenty-five Marine aircraft that had engaged the Japanese, only three returned undamaged, while seven others were shot up so badly that it was impossible to repair them. The other fifteen found a watery grave a few miles off the reef. Major Parks's was among them.

Colonel Shannon, painfully conscious that his fighters had not been able to hold back Tomonaga's bombers, had been standing at his command post watching the sky to the west.

"Open fire when targets are in range!" he shouted.

It was then about 6:30. A minute or two later the first of Midway's guns spat out its defiance, driving the island's sea birds into headlong flight. Quickly other guns opened fire and soon projectiles were being rammed into the breeches of all six 3-inch antiaircraft batteries, spotting the morning sky with bursts of gray smoke. As Tomonaga came nearer, smaller batteries opened up with a discordant clatter, raking the air with tracer bullets. The Japanese pilots could see and feel the intensity of the enfilade, for after the strike they were to tell Nagumo that the opposing gunfire had been vicious. But neither the gallant Marine fighter pilots nor their brothers on the ground were able to impede the enemy.

At 6:35 the Japanese bombers were over Midway, with no fighters to oppose them. One flight winged over Sand Island to the left, on whose northeastern shore were barracks, a large hangar, seaplane ramps, and fuel storage tanks. Another flight pushed over to smaller Eastern Island to the right, where were located the triangulated runways for land-based planes and a Marine mess hall and galley. The huge bombs tumbled down and detonated all along the northern shores of both islands. One bomb crashed into the seaplane hangar, setting it afire; another tore through a huge fuel storage tank, creating an inferno and sending fat clouds of black smoke skyward. One explosion ripped open the dispensary; others made great craters in the sand. On Eastern

Island a bomb shattered the mess hall, another crashed into a command post, killing the sector commander, Major William W. Benson, and wounding many of the men who were with him.

The powerhouse on Eastern Island was demolished, and a seaman, C. J. Stanfield, on watch there, lifted a badly wounded sailor on his back and carried him to the First Aid Station, despite the fact that bombs were still falling and strafing planes were making runs across the island. By now many storehouses were in flames, and the whole western part of the atoll was blanketed with clouds of heavy smoke which drifted westward with the wind. One missile hurtled into the Post Exchange, erupting in a cloud of razor blades, cigarettes, and candy bars. An enemy bomber pilot tore across Eastern Island at an altitude of fifty feet, rolled over in a flaunting stunt, and thumbed his nose.

In ten minutes the attack was over and Tomonaga reformed his planes for the return flight, radioing Nagumo at 6:45:

WE HAVE COMPLETED OUR ATTACK AND ARE HOMEWARD BOUND.

The next order of business for both sides was the assessment of damage received and inflicted. In the heat of battle there are often inaccurate counts of enemy planes knocked out of the sky. So it was at Midway, with American and Japanese observers alike "seeing" things which were not there. Tomonaga's pilots claimed to have shot down forty-two American planes, when actually only twenty-five fighters engaged them. American estimates of Japanese aircraft losses are also at variance with one another: one suggests that almost half the planes of the Japanese strike were shot down, while other estimates are less excessive. The fact is, nonetheless, that Tomonaga did unload his bombs and most of his pilots lived to tell about it.[2]

As his flight was regaining its formation, Tomonaga had a few minutes to assess the damage his strike had wrought. He had killed very few men in the raid, a fact which would have held not the slightest interest for him had he been able to know about it, but there were several matters he did know about which gave him some concern. The Marine antiaircraft fire had been spirited, and although he was confident that his pilots had disabled some of Midway's gun emplacements, the volume of fire which continued during his departure convinced him that too many Marine guns were still operable. Furthermore, because of the unenviable marksmanship of some of his bombers, the runways which he had hoped to destroy were still intact. The raid, therefore, had not been entirely successful and at 7 o'clock he sent another message to Nagumo:

THERE IS NEED FOR A SECOND ATTACK WAVE.

Up to this time Admiral Nagumo had been cautious, having kept more than a hundred planes on board his carriers in case one of his search planes should happen to sight a force of American ships. Tomonaga's urgent message nudged Nagumo into a vague uneasiness. If he sent his reserve planes off on another strike at Midway, he would be utterly defenseless. Should American land-based or carrier-borne aircraft find him in this condition, he knew disaster would be inevitable. Yet if he did not cripple Midway's air power, then it might be Admiral Tanaka's invasion troopships which would be doomed. Nor could he linger too long under the clear sky, for he knew that while Tomonaga had been winging toward Midway his carriers had been shadowed by several Catalinas. The Americans, therefore, had his position pin-pointed, and even if there were no hostile ships in the immediate vicinity, there was always the possibility of a submarine attack.

It is always easy for analysts to reflect on the "bad decisions" made in a naval battle, and Nagumo did not escape criticism for what he ultimately did. Yet his position was almost untenable, and was further aggravated when some minutes later another radio message was received, sent by the air officer of the carrier *Kaga,* who was flying with the returning attack group.

SAND ISLAND BOMBED, AND GREAT RESULTS OBTAINED.

Whatever prompted *Kaga's* air officer to transmit this jubilant and misleading message is not known. By this time, though, another aspect of the battle was developing, which was to convince Nagumo that Tomonaga's report was right, the other one a bit too imaginative.

About 7:15 at Midway, Lieutenant Colonel Ira L. Kimes, head of the Marine Aircraft Group, broadcast a message to the planes which had flown off with Parks and Armistead.

FIGHTERS LAND, REFUEL BY DIVISIONS, 5TH DIVISION FIRST.

He waited for an answer, but none came. Then he radioed several times:

ALL FIGHTERS LAND AND RESERVICE.

Once more he waited but, as we have seen, very few came back. In the meantime, however, other aircraft—Army, Navy and Marine Corps—which had left Midway at various times before the Japanese attack, were closing in on Nagumo. At about the time that he was learning that Sand Island had been bombed with "great results," there was the blare of a bugle warning of an air raid. Instantly signals were run up on halyards, engineroom annunciators clanged for more speed, gunners leaped to their stations, and all eyes stared at the southeastern sky, watching the four Army B-26's and the six Navy TBF's in two mixed waves stream in for a torpedo attack. The screening destroyers opened fire, and then the aircraft of Nagumo's combat air patrol, which had been circling the fleet, dove down like hawks, machine guns blazing. By now, with helm spun around to full rudder, the *Akagi* was turning toward the attacking planes. The Army and Navy pilots flew in through the spray of hot steel, maneuvering for an attack course. Hardly had they reached their release point when three of them, hit squarely, nosed over and plunged into the sea. Another aircraft was suddenly tailed by a swarm of Zeros, and before the pilot could launch his torpedo he was driven off by the murderous crossfire. The remaining six planes now faced the fire of every Japanese gun that could be trained on them. Three burst into flames as the enemy gunners found the mark; the others released their torpedoes, but the lead plane, now hit and out of control, soared over the *Akagi's* flight deck, barely missing the bridge, and crashed into the sea in a flash of fire. Only one Navy and two Army aircraft survived the attack and managed to get back to base.

The torpedoes had been dropped so far out and had traveled toward their targets at such slow speed that the enemy ships were able to twist away from their glistening wakes. Nagumo watched the white tracks pass along the port side of his flagship, and the sight convinced him that a second strike at Midway had to be ordered. So the gallant torpedo attack, while it inflicted no damage on Nagumo's ships, forced him into a command decision.

Immediately after the torpedo attack was repelled, Nagumo drafted the following order for his reserve aircraft:

PLANES IN SECOND ATTACK WAVE STAND BY TO CARRY OUT ATTACK TODAY. RE-EQUIP YOURSELVES WITH BOMBS.

This sudden change of plans required a considerable amount of carrier gymnastics. If Nagumo's reserve aircraft had not been armed for an attack on American surface ships, he might have been able to launch all of them at once, thus clearing his decks for the returning flight, which was due to arrive at about 8:30. But some of these planes had been held in readiness for an entirely different mission, which explains why those of the *Akagi* and *Kaga* were armed with torpedoes. They therefore had to be sent below to the hangar deck so that the torpedoes could be replaced with bombs. Such an operation required feverish activity on the part of the plane handlers and ordnancemen, and at just about the time that the change would be completed Tomonaga, low on gas and probably nursing some cripples in his flock, would be gliding into the landing circle and would have to be taken aboard.

Nagumo's problem, then, reduced itself to a race against time. If the rearming of the torpedo-laden aircraft on *Akagi* and *Kaga* could be done quickly, he might yet be able to get his second strike wave launched before Tomonaga arrived. If not, then his decks would have to be cleared for the recovery of the first attack wave. Thus Admiral Nagumo placed himself in jeopardy, even though, for the moment, he felt safe. There were a number of Zeros circling overhead on combat air patrol, and he still had the tremendous fire power of his two battleships, three cruisers and eleven destroyers which were steaming with him. The accuracy of Japanese gunnery during the recent ill-fated American torpedo attack had been most cheering.

It was 7:15 when Nagumo flashed his order to the air groups. Sailors began wheeling planes to the elevators and taking them below, where the torpedoes were disengaged. Heavy bombs were then lifted from their storage cradles in the magazines and lugged into position beneath the belly of each aircraft. The pilots, with an hour's reprieve, lounged about the ready room, waiting to be called for the second attack on the atoll. From his flag bridge Nagumo watched the furious activity on the flight deck. He would have halted it instantly had he known what was happening less than 200 miles to the northeast of him. For Admiral Spruance had reached his launching position, and a few minutes after 7 o'clock, at just about the time when Nagumo was beating off the last of the attacking torpedo planes, the first aircraft were leaving the flight decks of the American carriers *Enterprise* and *Hornet*.

Although a great many American aircraft had been shot down during the early hours of the morning, including scout planes, fighters and torpedo bombers, Nagumo still did not believe that an enemy carrier force was in the area. However, he had taken the normal precaution of sending a number of scout planes aloft to warn him in case of a miscalculation in Japanese naval intelligence. These aircraft were still flying about on their appointed patrols when he ordered the second Midway strike.

At 7:28, while the rearming was going on at a heated pace, Nagumo received a shattering message. The search plane from the cruiser *Tone*—the one whose launching had been delayed by about thirty minutes—had reached the 300-mile limit of its outbound easterly flight and had turned northward on the short 60-mile leg of its search pattern. Suddenly the pilot spotted what appeared to be a formation of ships far ahead and to the left of him. As he drew nearer he counted the vessels and made a hurried estimate of their position, course and speed. Then he flashed the news to Nagumo:

SIGHT WHAT APPEARS TO BE TEN ENEMY SURFACE SHIPS, BEARING 010°, 240 MILES FROM MIDWAY. COURSE 150°, SPEED OVER 20 KNOTS.

Vital minutes were squandered while a staff officer plotted the information and Nagumo tried to make up his mind what to do. His task was not an easy one. This was the first he had learned of the presence of enemy ships in the area. They were, moreover, in sufficient number to comprise a task force, and their reported position placed them within air striking distance of the Japanese carriers. The information was extremely valuable, but Nagumo was annoyed with its brevity, especially since the reporting pilot had failed to say what type of ships he had so fortunately sighted. The message intruded upon Nagumo's previous calm at a most unfavorable time. He became sullen and, what was far worse, indecisive.

For a quarter of an hour he paced the bridge, weighing possibilities. If the *Tone* pilot had given the enemy's course with reasonable accuracy, then the enemy ships were not even heading for him. But suppose they suddenly changed course to the right? What then? Furthermore, if the force consisted of only cruisers and destroyers and perhaps a battleship or two, he would still have a large margin of time on his side, for even should the sighted ships succeed in bending on a sustained speed of 30 knots or more, they could not possibly get within range for a gun duel for another six hours. However, Japanese intelligence had known long beforehand that Nimitz had two, possibly three, aircraft carriers available. If even one of these was steaming with the enemy formation, then Nagumo was in serious peril, for it meant that American carrier-based planes were at that very moment within striking distance of his ships. The blunders inherent in Yamamoto's imperious strategy were now beclouding the scene. Nagumo had to commit himself to two uncongenial actions—to hit Midway and to fight an enemy fleet. It was a tragedy for Nagumo and a blessing for Fletcher and Spruance that these two actions demanded simultaneous attention.

At 7:45 Nagumo broke through his indecision and issued another order:

PREPARE TO CARRY OUT ATTACKS ON ENEMY FLEET UNITS. LEAVE TORPEDOES ON THOSE ATTACK PLANES WHICH HAVE NOT AS YET BEEN CHANGED TO BOMBS.

Instantly the rearming operation was halted, but about half the job had been completed and there was no time to reverse the process. The attack, therefore, would have to be undertaken with half the usual number of torpedo planes. Again the aircraft which had been struck below were brought back to the flight decks, and squadron commanders briefed their pilots on the impending action. Nagumo continued to feel uneasy and at 7:47 he radioed a message to the *Tone* plane:

ASCERTAIN SHIP TYPES AND MAINTAIN CONTACT.

Eleven minutes later the *Tone* pilot sent another message to Nagumo, advising that the enemy ships were still making about 20 knots but that three minutes before (7:55) they had changed course to 080°. He included no information about ship types. Nagumo, impatient with the pilot, ordered another message sent at once:

Climax At Midway

At this point Nagumo's attention was diverted from the radio receiver to the sky. Because of the previous air attacks, he had ordered all his fighters aloft to bolster the combat air patrols which had been droning over the carriers all morning. Yet none of these planes was high enough in altitude to avert what was about to happen.

The sixteen Marine dive bombers, led by Major Henderson, had by this time moved into a favorable attack position. At a few minutes before 8 o'clock Henderson, flying at 9000 feet without a single fighter plane to protect him, pushed through the clouds and soon found the Japanese carriers. The enemy ships came alive. Bugles sounded, signal flags were hoisted, and the Zeros on patrol started to climb.

Henderson knew that his pilots were unfamiliar with the planes they were flying. An accidental explosion of a fuel storage tank at Midway before the battle had resulted in a severe curtailment of gasoline allowances which, in turn, had placed strict limits on flight training operations. Accordingly Henderson decided to avoid the tricky, steep dive-bombing attack in favor of a simpler glide approach. Dropping down to 4000 feet, he selected the *Akagi* as his target and began his attack while Nagumo's Zeros came up to meet him. Bullets ripped through Henderson's plane, flames spilled out of his cockpit, and his battered aircraft spiralled downward. Captain Elmer G. Glidden continued the attack, with each plane making its plunge at five-second intervals. Some of the aircraft, with controls shot away, dove headlong into the sea; others got close enough to release their bombs and then pulled out of their dives. The throat microphone of Lieutenant Daniel Iverson was shot clean away and his plane was riddled with over 250 bullet holes. But he was one of the lucky eight who survived the attack.

After making his glide, Captain Glidden kept low and headed for Midway with the mauled remains of Henderson's squadron. Nagumo had been taken by surprise, and he bowed with relief when he received word that none of his ships had been hit.[3] He was in the act of straightening out the lines of his fleet when another attack roared in.

Colonel Sweeney, who had led his Flying Fortresses toward Tanaka's transports until ordered by Midway to go after the Japanese carriers, was now soaring overhead at a height of almost four miles. From the bridge of the *Akagi*, Nagumo could see the *Kaga*, *Hiryu* and *Soryu*, far out of position because of their recent evasive maneuvers. Suddenly a torrent of explosives, more than four tons from each plane, hurtled toward the ships. Again rudders were put over hard, the engineroom telegraphs rattled and then jerked to *Full Speed Ahead.* Valves were spun open and orders sounded above the throbbing machinery.

With a crash the bombs hit, throwing up great columns of grayish water. The *Hiryu* was straddled; the *Soryu* put down a smoke screen which suggested for a brief moment that she had been hit. Guns were firing and the Japanese ships were weaving frantically to the left, then to the right, to avoid the shower of bombs.

The attack was over as suddenly as it had begun, and Sweeney returned to Midway, confident that he had scored hits on two of Nagumo's carriers. Actually, the Japanese

Carrier Striking Force was hit with nothing more than the spray from near misses. Nagumo was still safe.

During the air attacks which had taken place during the past hour or so, Nagumo's ships had been zigzagging wildly, and it had become quite impossible for him to launch the second attack wave, destined now not for Midway but for the recently sighted American surface force. The *Tone* pilot, in the meantime, having been told sternly at 8 o'clock to identify the enemy ships he was then shadowing, finally complied at 8:09 with the following message:

ENEMY IS COMPOSED OF FIVE CRUISERS AND FIVE DESTROYERS.

This news caused Nagumo untold relief. There were no carriers! The American ships sighted by the *Tone* aircraft could do him no harm so long as they remained beyond gun range, as they presently were. And if they held onto their new heading of 080°, they were opening the distance rather than closing it. Under these conditions Nagumo could direct an air strike against them later in the morning, almost at his leisure, with no immediate fear of being hit himself. He went back to his original plan of bombing Midway for a second time. The planes on the flight decks of *Hiryu* and *Soryu* were dive bombers, ready for launching; about half of *Akagi's* and *Kaga's* aircraft had had their torpedoes replaced with bombs and had been brought up again from the hangar deck. Collectively, these aircraft comprised quite a formidable striking force, and since the last of Henderson's bombers were being driven off about the same time that Nagumo was reading the reassuring message from the *Tone*

ADVERSARIES

Fleet Admiral Chester W. Nimitz, Commander in Chief, United States Pacific Fleet. A man of "monumental patience and optimism . . . indispensable to America's cause in the Pacific."

Vice Admiral Chuichi Nagumo, Commander, Japanese First Carrier Striking Force. After the battle of Midway he wrote: ". . . we participated in this operation with meager training and without knowledge of the enemy."

Vice Admiral Frank Jack Fletcher (Rear Admiral at the time of the battle of Midway and Commander, Task Force Seventeen). At its full strength this force included the two 20,000-ton aircraft carriers *Yorktown* and *Lexington,* eight cruisers, thirteen destroyers, and two fleet tankers.

Vice Admiral Raymond A. Spruance (Rear Admiral at the time of the battle of Midway and Commander, Task Force Sixteen): "He proved that leadership is not made in battle; it is only exhibited."

Above, left. Lieutenant Commander Clarence W. McClusky, Air Group Commander of the *Enterprise. Above, right.* Lieutenant James S. Gray.

Lieutenant Commander Eugene E. Lindsey.

Captain M. F. Leslie, as he appeared in 1948, six years after the battle of Midway.

Lieutenant Commander John C. Waldron, in command of USS *Hornet* Torpedo Squadron 8.

PBY-5A. It was this type of aircraft which first sighted the Japanese carriers headed toward Midway.

An SBD, Navy dive bomber. Slow, rugged, and dependable, it was in use before the war and was not replaced until near the end of the war.

A TBF in flight. One of the most versatile aircraft in World War II, it was designed as a torpedo bomber but was used for glide and horizontal bombing, search, and even cargo carrying.

USS *Enterprise,* flagship of Rear Admiral Raymond A. Spruance at the battle of Midway. The "Big-E," often battered, had one of the heroic careers of modern naval warfare.

USS *Yorktown* during the battle of Midway. A plane has just been launched from the flight deck.

Japanese Zero maneuvering to escape a barrage. USS *Yorktown* is at right.

Japanese planes attempt to attack U.S. Pacific Fleet forces through heavy antiaircraft fire. Smoke on the horizon is from an enemy bomber shot down. Splashes in the foreground are caused by falling shell fragments.

USS *Yorktown* burning. She went down at 6:00 a.m. on June 7, 1942.

Japanese heavy cruiser of the *Mogami* class on fire after attack by Task Force 16 planes.

search plane, he was able to revise his plans with supreme confidence. Although the sky was clear to the east, shielding clouds drifted above his head, his ships so far were undamaged, and no enemy carriers had been reported. He felt quite safe. He was able to enjoy this illusion for another eleven minutes.

At 8:20 the conservative pilot of the *Tone* plane was heard from once more.

THE ENEMY IS ACCOMPANIED BY WHAT APPEARS TO BE A CARRIER.

Even though identification was not positive, since the newly discovered enemy ship only "appeared" to be a carrier, Nagumo could not risk his own forces. The follow-up bombing of Midway, which he had just decided to undertake, had to be abandoned for a second time.

Again Nagumo was prevented from launching an immediate attack on the American ships, first because the remaining torpedo planes would have to be brought up from the hangar deck, and second because the eleven Marine level-bombers under Major Norris were just then flying over the Japanese formation. Before Norris could even begin his letdown he was attacked by several Zeros from Nagumo's air combat patrol, but he managed to lead his sluggish aircraft into the clouds and shake off the enemy fighters. A few moments later he came down to 2000 feet. The clouds opened up and he found himself, unfortunately, just over the battleship *Haruna*, which was steaming a considerable distance from the Japanese carriers. If he wasted valuable moments in search of the carriers he might be shot down without hitting anything, so Norris decided to attack the big ship below him. At that moment the *Haruna* opened fire and each Marine pilot, as he began his glide, was followed down by machine-gunning Zeros. These young Marine pilots, like Henderson's men before them, dove into the attack with not a single fighter to cover them. It is understandable why they scored no hits on the Japanese battleship, although they are credited with downing two enemy aircraft. For the time being, Norris was luckier than Henderson. After the brief attack was over, nine of his fliers made their way back to Midway.

While this attack was ending, Lieutenant Commander William H. Brockman, skipper of the submarine *Nautilus*, was patrolling on a bearing of 310° from Midway. He had been attacked with depth charges about twenty minutes before, but at 8:20 he came to periscope depth to see if he could find a target. He found ships on all sides, racing across his field of vision in frantic evasive movements. He could see flags being run up and signal lights flashing warnings. Then a battleship on his port bow, with a high, cluttered pagoda mast, swung its big guns toward Brockman's periscope and opened fire. With lightning speed Brockman calculated a torpedo collision course and sent one speeding on its way toward the target; the battleship put her rudder over hard, turning away from the *Nautilus,* and Brockman missed. Diving deep, he rigged his boat for a depth-charge attack which was not long in coming. Brockman managed to survive this crashing attack, and when he raised his periscope again at 8:46, Nagumo's Striking Force had disappeared. Only a lone destroyer remained behind to hunt for him. While the enemy ship sounded into the depths with its echo-ranging gear, Brockman pulled away carefully and thus avoided another hammering from depth charges.

By 8:30, although Nagumo had been attacked by Flying Fortresses, torpedo planes, dive bombers and a submarine, his ships were still unharmed. It seemed as though the gods were truly smiling on him, but then the *Tone* search plane supplemented its previous message:

SIGHT TWO ADDITIONAL ENEMY CRUISERS IN POSITION BEARING 080°, DISTANCE 250 MILES FROM MIDWAY. COURSE 150°, SPEED 20 KNOTS.

The enemy now had seven cruisers, five destroyers and possibly an aircraft carrier! It was painfully clear to Nagumo that he would have to launch an attack against this force without a moment's delay, but he found himself trapped by the results of his earlier hesitation. The only aircraft that were properly armed for such a strike against the American ships were the bombers nested on the flight decks of *Hiryu* and *Soryu* and the torpedo planes of *Akagi* and *Kaga* which had not yet been rearmed with bombs. It was not a well-balanced force, but it was all Nagumo had to work with at the moment. What is more, it suffered from a serious deficiency—it had no fighters, since Nagumo had sent them all off to repel the persistent air attacks of Midway-based planes. With half-empty fuel tanks, the Zeros could not be expected to escort the bombers and torpedo planes, and to send the flight off without fighter protection would be suicidal. Nagumo had already witnessed the slaughter of the Navy's TBF's, the Army's B-26's, and the Marine Corps' bombers, all of them unescorted by fighter aircraft.

Nagumo was caught in a web of events over which he had no control. Unwilling to risk the lives of his pilots, he suddenly committed himself to a course of action from which there was no turning back. He decided to hit the American force with a "full load" of torpedo planes, bombers and fighters. This meant that his air-borne fighter planes, with the exception of those comprising a normal air combat patrol, would have to be recovered, rearmed and refueled. At 8:30, as he was about to issue his command, Tomonaga's incoming flight was sighted.

Once more Nagumo was confronted with an urgent need to change his plans, and his logic as well as his resolution began to wilt. The flight decks had to be cleared so that Tomonaga's flight could land. Nagumo could clear the decks in two ways: launch the waiting bombers and torpedo planes without fighter protection, or order the planes below to the hangar deck. He elected the second way, and after most of the waiting planes were moved off the flight decks, Tomonaga was instructed to land.

Rear Admiral Tamon Yamaguchi, second in command of the carrier force and flying his flag from the *Hiryu's* mast, could not understand what his senior was doing. He, too, had been intercepting the various contact reports transmitted by the *Tone* search plane and he was not at all reassured by them. It was by no means clear to him why his chief was delaying an air strike at the enemy force, and although it is not often wise for a junior admiral to advise his senior what to do, Yamaguchi felt that a serious danger was lurking beyond the northeastern horizon and, fighters or no fighters, Nagumo should try to neutralize it instantly. Therefore he drafted a message to be relayed to the *Akagi*.

CONSIDER IT ADVISABLE TO LAUNCH ATTACK FORCE IMMEDIATELY.[4]

Nagumo did not concur.

Again maintenance crews lowered planes to the hangar decks, and those aircraft which had first been armed with torpedoes and then rearmed with bombs, were once more being armed with torpedoes. The enlisted men who had to make these seemingly pointless changes worked with furious haste, and there were probably a few of them who thought that the war had begun to push Nagumo over the line of sanity.

Akagi recovered her first planes at 8:37, and while Tomonaga's aircraft were being landed and struck below, the search plane shadowing the American surface force was running out of gas. The pilot flashed a message to Nagumo:

I AM HOMEWARD BOUND.

Nagumo answered at 8:54.

GO ON THE AIR WITH TRANSMITTER FOR DF (direction finding) PURPOSES.

If Nagumo was apparently satisfied to leave the enemy ships unwatched, Rear Admiral Hiroaki Abe was not. Riding in the *Tone,* flagship of Cruiser Division Eight, Abe sent a two-part message to the search plane:

POSTPONE YOUR HOMING,

MAINTAIN CONTACT WITH ENEMY UNTIL ARRIVAL OF FOUR CHIKUMA PLANES. GO ON THE AIR WITH YOUR LONG-WAVE TRANSMITTER.

While these words were being hammered out in the cruiser's radio room, the search plane advised Nagumo that ten enemy torpedo planes were heading for the Japanese carriers. The sea was calm, brushed by only a gentle wind, but the planes were not spotted from the flag bridge of the *Akagi,* where signal lights were hastily spelling out Nagumo's belated decision to attack.

AFTER COMPLETING LANDING OPERATIONS PROCEED NORTHWARD. WE PLAN TO CONTACT AND DESTROY THE ENEMY TASK FORCE.

The message was relayed to all ships and within a few minutes every commanding officer knew what his next move was to be.

Nagumo also sent a radio dispatch to Yamamoto, who was far to the west, unable to render any immediate help.

ENEMY COMPOSED OF 1 CARRIER, 5 CRUISERS AND 5 DESTROYERS SIGHTED AT 5 A.M.[5] POSITION BEARING 010°, DISTANCE 240 MILES FROM MIDWAY. WE ARE HEADING FOR IT.

It was a curious dispatch, full of errors and misinformation, for the enemy force had been sighted at 7:28 (4:28 Tokyo time), the position given was the first one reported by the *Tone* aircraft at 7:28, and the "two additional cruisers" reported at 8:30, twenty-five minutes before the dispatch went on the air, were not even mentioned. Such a dispatch can only be explained by the fact that Nagumo had spent a very difficult morning reading a succession of disturbing dispatches, dodging bombs and torpedoes, and making command decisions on which he had had to reverse himself several times. His anxiety was mounting as he waited for the last fighter planes to come in. It was enough for Yamamoto to know that he was about to attack the enemy force. The precise details were not so very important.

At 9:18 the last plane touched down on the *Akagi's* flight deck and Nagumo immediately swung his ships around to a northeasterly heading and set fleet speed at 30 knots. The big Japanese carriers left churning wakes behind them as they pointed their bows northward. Below the flight decks a frantic struggle was going on to get the planes armed, fueled and readied for attack. But almost immediately enemy aircraft were sighted and Nagumo again had to resort to evasive maneuvers while some of his supporting ships laid down a billowing smoke screen. Admiral Spruance had followed Fletcher's orders to "proceed southwesterly and attack enemy carriers when definitely located," and his thunderbolts were soon to fall on the Japanese fleet.

For Nagumo the magic spell was broken.

CHAPTER
6

~~~~~~~~

DEATH OF THE
TORPEDO PLANES

*The standards were now raised on both
sides, and the two fleets met and
fought . . . The engagement was obsti-
nate, but more courage than skill was displayed, and it had almost the appearance
of a battle by land.*

THUCYDIDES: *Peloponnesian War*

EARLY THAT MORNING, even before Tomonaga informed Nagumo that a second strike at Midway was necessary, Admiral
Spruance's Task Force Sixteen was ready for battle. For
almost an hour the *Enterprise* and *Hornet* had been steaming at 25 knots on a course of 240°. All the Catalina contact
reports transmitted during the early hours of the morning
had come under Spruance's critical gaze, and from them he
derived a fairly accurate idea of Nagumo's position, course
and speed. By projecting the Japanese course line, he was

able to forecast all probable future positions of the enemy carriers as they moved toward Midway. He also reasoned that Nagumo, taking advantage of the prevailing winds, would for some time continue on his present course to recover his incoming planes.

By this time, too, the *Yorktown's* search planes were back on board and Admiral Fletcher, his task force just coming over the northern horizon, was following in Spruance's wake. The *Yorktown's* deck was spotted with twelve torpedo planes under Lieutenant Commander Lance E. Massey, seventeen dive bombers in two groups led by Lieutenant Commander Maxwell F. Leslie and Lieutenant Wallace C. Short, Jr., and six fighters under Lieutenant Commander John S. Thach. This was by no means *Yorktown's* full air strength, but Fletcher wanted to protect himself should another enemy carrier be lurking under the clouded horizon to the west of him. Admiral Spruance, to be sure, was steaming toward a target which American scout planes had identified positively as Japanese, but these enemy ships, so far as Fletcher was concerned, might be merely part of a more diffused attack force. For this reason he did not launch his own aircraft immediately but chose to wait a little longer, in case a subsequent contact report should warn him that his starboard flank was threatened.

In any case, the first American carrier-borne aircraft to strike the enemy were the torpedo planes. Although the torpedo squadrons from the *Yorktown* and *Enterprise* were as much deserving of laurels as were the pilots who flew with *Hornet's* Lieutenant Commander John C. Waldron, it was Waldron's exploit which stirred the nation.

Hornet's Torpedo Squadron Eight, consisting of fifteen pilots and an equal number of tail gunners,[1] carried a reputation for eccentricity, and this was due in no small part to the personality and character of Waldron. Born in South Dakota, he was graduated from Annapolis on 4 June 1924, and three years later won his wings as a naval aviator. Early in August, 1941, he took over command of Torpedo Squadron Eight.

One of Waldon's great grandparents was a Sioux, and he liked to rely as much on his Indian intuition as his professional experience in preparing his pilots for aerial warfare. During the months preceding the battle, Waldron scrounged from naval supply depots a whole assortment of equipment —hunting knives, small pocket compasses, and even steel bucket seats with high backs to protect his pilots from small-calibre machine-gun fire. When in San Diego and San Francisco he bought up large sheets of leather, carted them on board and then put his pilots to work fashioning knife sheaths and shoulder holsters. With a .45 automatic tucked under the left shoulder, another dangling from the right hip, and a hunting knife strapped to their belts, Waldron's fliers looked like a band of revolutionaries. Other aviators were amused at this display of personal armament, but Waldron brushed aside their good-natured derision. To his own pilots he explained, "You can never tell when you'll be forced down in some jungle. If that ever happens to you, this stuff will come in handy." It was not long before the scoffers changed their minds about Waldron's precautions and imitated him.

Waldron loved the officers and men under his command

but, being a natural leader, he was careful not to show it. He kept his pilots flying for long hours, and when the weather was inclement he limbered them up with calisthenics or ushered them into the ready room to work out tactical problems.

Often the officers grumbled about the pace Waldron had set for them, but in time they came to understand his fierce devotion to the squadron and took his extracurricular assignments in stride. Waldron, they knew, had transformed them into an élite fraternity; they were ready in body and mind for any challenge. And through the weeks and months of incessant training and drills they found something else in Waldron, a courage from which all of them were able to draw strength.

Before the attack, Waldron wrote two letters. To his wife he said:

"Dearest Adelaide:

"There is not a bit of news that I can tell you except that I am well. I have yours and the children's pictures here with me all the time. . . .

"I believe that we will be in battle very soon—I wish we were there today. But as we are up to the very eve of serious business, I wish to record to you that I am feeling fine. My own morale is excellent and from my continued observance of the squadron—their morale is excellent also. You may rest assured that I will go in with the expectation of coming back in good shape. If I do not come back—well, you and the little girls can know that this squadron struck for the highest objective in naval warfare— 'To Sink the Enemy.'

". . . I love you and the children very dearly and I long to be with you. But I could not be happy ashore at this time. My place is here with the fight . . . I know you wish me luck and I believe I will have it.

"You know, Adelaide, in this business of the torpedo attack, I acknowledge we must have a break. I believe that I have the experience and enough Sioux in me to recognize the break when it comes—and it will come.

". . . God bless you dear. You are a wonderful wife and mother. Kiss and love the little girls for me and be of good cheer.

"Love to all from Daddy and Johnny."

The other letter he wrote to the squadron and appended it to his attack plan. It read:

"Just a word to let you know I feel we are ready. We have had a very short time to train and we have worked under the most severe difficulties. But we have truly done the best humanly possible. I actually believe that under these conditions we are the best in the world. My greatest hope is that we encounter a favorable tactical situation, but if we don't, and the worst comes to the worst, I want each of us to do his utmost to destroy our enemies. If there is only one plane left to make a final run in, I want that man to go in and get a hit. May God be with all of us. Good luck, happy landings and give 'em hell."

Waldron waited while the last star faded and the rising sun washed the highest cloud clusters with light. The contact reports had come in like fragments of a strangely incoherent conversation. Yesterday's reality, heavy with tension, was replaced by today's, giving to the impending strike the aspect of an imaginary adventure. Some men could feel a personal exhilaration, others felt anger, a few pretended to joke. All were alone.

The morning wind blew in from the southeast. Planes were fueled and armed. Then came the whine of starters, and propellers began to spin for the warmup, washing a stream of blue exhaust sternward. The bridge areas of the *Enterprise* and the *Hornet* were crowded with officers and men. Pilots, answering the call to "Flight Quarters," filled the ready rooms, where they heard last-minute instructions from their squadron commanders as teletypes clicked out the latest information on the Japanese Striking Force. The enemy's position was then estimated to be 155 sea miles away on a bearing of 239°. It did not take much arithmetic for Waldron to figure out that his heavily-laden torpedo planes, under these conditions, would not have enough fuel to return to the *Hornet*. But the strike had to be made, and he could only hope that he and his men would be rescued by a seaplane or a destroyer when the battle was over. Just before launching time, he climbed to the bridge, reported to Captain Mitscher for final instructions and informed him that he would attack the enemy "regardless of consequences." Remembering that last farewell, Mitscher was later to write:

"His grim determination to press home an attack against all obstacles, his foreknowledge that there was the possibility that his squadron was doomed to destruction with no chance whatever of returning safely to the carrier, impressed all present with the remarkable devotion to duty and the personal integrity of an officer whose pilots asked only that they be allowed to share in the dangers and disastrous fate sure to follow such an attack."

Thirty-five of *Hornet's* bombers, with a mixed load of 1000- and 500-pound bombs, were readied for take-off. Behind them would come Waldron's fifteen torpedo planes and Lieutenant Commander Samuel G. Mitchell's fighter escort of ten aircraft, loaded only with machine-gun ammunition. The bombers were divided into Bombing Squadron Eight, under Lieutenant Commander Robert R. Johnson, and Scouting Squadron Eight, under Lieutenant Commander Walter F. Rodee. This strike—sixty aircraft in all—was to be led by Commander Stanhope C. Ring, *Hornet's* Air Group Commander.

Nearby, the *Enterprise's* thirty-seven bombers, commanded by Lieutenants Richard H. Best and Wilmer E. Gallaher, were being readied. Behind them rested Lieutenant Commander Eugene E. Lindsey's fourteen torpedo planes, backed up by Lieutenant James S. Gray's ten fighters. Lieutenant Commander Clarence W. McClusky would lead the attack.

Just before 7 o'clock, while Nagumo's planes were returning from Midway, Admiral Spruance turned Task Force Sixteen into the wind. At 7 the *Hornet's* first aircraft sped down the flight deck and lifted slowly into the light breeze. A few minutes later the *Enterprise* launched her first plane and

Death of the Torpedo Planes

Spruance's air strike of sixty bombers, twenty-nine torpedo planes and twenty fighters was rising into the wind.

The first bombers climbed for altitude; then they winged over into orbit, awaiting the arrival of their fellows. The air trembled with the thrum of twenty, thirty, forty aircraft.

In the ready room Waldron explained to his pilots the formation he wished to maintain on the outbound flight—six sections of two aircraft, one section of three. Waldron would be in the lead, and a twenty-five-year-old Texan, Ensign George Gay, would ride at the tail of the formation. As the pilots climbed the ladder to the flight deck, Waldron spoke to Gay:

"Tex, don't worry about your navigation. I think the Japs will change course. Just keep on my tail and I'll take you to them." [2]

While the last bombers were roaring along the flight decks, lookouts sighted *Tone's* search plane, and Admiral Spruance knew that his decision to launch early had been right. The Japanese would now know his position and ultimately the position of Admiral Fletcher, who was still holding back his planes to meet a challenge possibly still concealed behind the western horizon. The sudden appearance of this enemy aircraft deeply concerned Spruance. McClusky was in the air with *Enterprise's* bombers; Lindsey's vulnerable torpedo planes were not yet airborne; and Tomonaga's Midway air strike was somewhere between the smoking atoll and Nagumo's carriers. But precisely where? It was also possible that a second Japanese attack wave was driving hard toward Midway. If the pilot of the enemy search plane managed to alert the Japanese admiral to the presence of

American carriers, would not Nagumo at that very instant be diverting his second attack wave from its southeasterly course and ordering it northeastward to bomb Task Force Sixteen?

There was no time for speculation, and Spruance ordered *Enterprise's* dive bombers to move out without the fighters or torpedo planes. Just before 8 o'clock McClusky's aircraft were little more than specks against the southern sky.

A few minutes later *Hornet's* bombers and fighters followed McClusky's southwesterly course toward that hypothetical point where Nagumo was expected to be when the attack began. Lieutenant Gray, leading *Enterprise's* fighters, circled above the task force waiting for the torpedo planes to climb into formation. Waldron, with his fifteen torpedo planes flying low at 300 feet, headed out on a course considerably to the right of the one taken by *Enterprise's* McClusky and *Hornet's* Ring; and nearby were Lindsey's torpedo planes moving out on a line that at first seemed to parallel Waldron's but later diverged slightly to the left. Gray, in the meantime, had to put his faster fighter aircraft through continuous "S" turns to avoid pulling too far ahead of the torpedo squadrons, both of which he had in sight for a good part of the outbound flight.

Meanwhile Admiral Fletcher, still uneasy about that sector of the sea off his starboard beam, decided to launch part of his air strike and hold the rest in readiness. Just after 9 o'clock the last plane of his air strike roared off into the southwestern sky, heading, like those from the *Enterprise* and *Hornet,* for the expected point of interception. But Nagumo did not hold to his course, a fact which almost led to

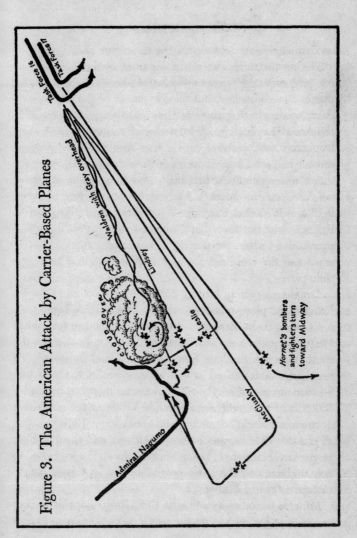

Figure 3. The American Attack by Carrier-Based Planes

Task Force 16
Task Force 17

Waldron with Gray overhead

Lindsey

CLOUD COVER

Leslie

Hornet's bombers and fighters turn toward Midway

McClusky

Admiral Nagumo

an overwhelming disaster for the American Fleet.

The geometric center of the Japanese Striking Force was roughly about 145 miles away when the last of Spruance's planes were launched, but the movement of the enemy carriers, while altering their relative position with respect to the American air strike, did not affect the range greatly since Nagumo's southeasterly course was approximately perpendicular to Task Force Sixteen's outbound flight. Allowing for minor miscalculations, McClusky and Ring could expect to converge on the enemy's Midway-bound carriers between 9:15 and 9:30 that morning. What threw everything out of balance was the fact that Nagumo—just as Waldron had prophesied—after recovering his aircraft, turned northward and therefore did not appear at the point of interception.

Commander Ring, leading *Hornet's* bombers and fighters, reached the place where the enemy should have been, and, not finding them there, flew on his original course for a little longer to make sure that Nagumo was not farther to the south than the previous contact reports had indicated. To his right clouds drifted in the morning sunlight; ahead was a broad stretch of empty ocean. A decision had to be made: Ring could turn, with equal gamble, either to the northwest or southeast along Nagumo's estimated course, for it was just as possible that he was between Midway and the Japanese carriers as they were between him and the atoll. He elected to take a chance on the latter possibility and so turned southeastward toward Midway.

Minutes ticked away and with them Ring's hope of finding the enemy, for the sea on the new heading was also barren of ships. Later he sighted the black smoke from Midway's burning fuel tanks and knew that he had lost the toss. Some of his planes got back to the *Hornet*, but thirteen of his bombers, running out of gas, had to touch down at Midway. They jettisoned their bombs offshore, and the battered defenders leaped to the alert as the air-raid siren sent out a false alarm. Eleven planes made the runway and were refueled, two landed in the lagoon, throwing up clouds of spray, and the fighters, their engines sputtering, splashed one by one into the sea. The bombers which landed safely were refueled and sent out again to locate the enemy, but their search was fruitless and they landed back on board the *Hornet* that afternoon.

McClusky, leading *Enterprise*'s strike, also passed the interception point without coming upon Nagumo's carriers, and therefore found himself in precisely the same predicament as Ring. After flying a considerable distance beyond where the Japanese carriers were expected to be, he decided to risk a search *away* from Midway, and thus turned his bombers toward the northwest. For McClusky—and for the final outcome of the battle—this was to be a most fortunate command decision, since the new course, as will be seen, brought him to within visual distance of the enemy.

Meanwhile Waldron, having gambled that Nagumo would change course, was spearheading his flight directly toward the Japanese Striking Force, while Lindsey, driving hard on Waldron's port quarter, was closing the enemy too, a few miles to the south of Torpedo Squadron Eight. Gray's fighters, flying 20,000 feet above the sea, zigzagged over the torpedo planes as they sped to the target. Gray had agreed upon a battle signal with *Enterprise's* torpedo squadron: when the attack run was about to begin, Lindsey's group would call Gray down from his high altitude, and he would break through the clouds, throttle wide open, and engage any Japanese fighters which attempted to break up the torpedo attack.

As the planes moved out, Gray had positioned himself above and slightly behind the leading torpedo squadron (Waldron's), and had the other one (Lindsey's) in plain view for the first part of the outbound flight. But after they were on their way, Gray and his pilots had to divide their time between making frequent "S" turns and keeping alert for Japanese Zeros, whose calling card was generally a sudden withering blast of machine-gun fire. A few minutes after 9 o'clock Gray approached a blanket of clouds which hung about 800 feet above the sea. Winging over, he saw far below him one squadron of torpedo planes just about to move under the cloud cover. He had time to count fifteen planes and knew that it was Waldron's squadron since Lindsey's had only fourteen aircraft. He was sure that Lindsey's group was close by, since its initial course had not been widely divergent from Waldron's. So Gray proceeded on course and waited for the prearranged signal to attack. Suddenly over the clouds he sighted several Japanese screening destroyers, and a few minutes later some larger vessels. This was journey's end, but since he had just lost the torpedo planes under the clouds, there was nothing for him to do but wait for Lindsey's signal. He decided, while waiting, to turn his fighters into a broad circle in search of McClusky's bombers.

Waldron had followed his hunch to the end of the line

and was rewarded when, glancing over his right wing, he sighted the outer screen of Nagumo's ships. His instincts had brought him to the very fringe of the enemy fleet. Immediately he adjusted his course slightly to the right and prepared to attack. As the squadron veered around and settled on the approach course, every man became an island, intense, incommunicative, and yet stubbornly loyal to Waldron from whom, even in the face of impending violence, they were able to draw courage.

The aircraft carrier directly ahead of Waldron was about eight miles away, less than five minutes' flying time. He gave the signal for the descent and the squadron nosed down to within a few yards of the surface of the sea. The enemy's destroyer screen was plainly visible as it twisted to the right to meet the attack, but the horizon at this lower altitude hid the Japanese carriers on the far side of the formation and only their masts and superstructures sprouted above the thin line separating the sea from the gray, infinite space beyond.

The enemy ships, catching the flash of sunlight on the wings of the torpedo planes, were zigzagging in emergency turns. Beyond the destroyers Waldron could see two carriers, one to the left, the other to the right of him. Directly in front was another carrier, and to the north of it he sighted what appeared to be a battleship. He elected to attack the nearest carrier, but about fifty Japanese fighter planes, which had been circling above the formation, were already plunging down at him from their high altitudes. Waldron issued commands and talked to his pilots, and his voice reached even Ring's southbound bombers.

"Johnny One to Johnny Two . . . See that splash . . . How am I doing . . . Attack immediately . . . There are two fighters in the water . . . My two wingmen are going in the water. . . ." [3]

The Zeros reached Waldron long before he got to his release point. Their blazing machine guns tore holes in the torpedo planes, making them swerve off course: as one fighter pulled out, another dove in. In a matter of seconds a third of the unprotected and hopelessly outnumbered squadron crashed into the sea. At a speed of 100 knots the impact was appalling. Rear-seatmen were crushed by hurtling machine guns; pilots were slammed against instrument panels and were dead before the sea poured into the cockpit. Others died in flight, their bodies ripped open by enemy bullets, and a few before they died had to endure agony as gasoline flames tore at their faces and blinded them.

To those who were still flying, the scene was frightful in its suddenness and finality. Gay, flying in the last position, could see each plane fall. The Zeros were thick overhead and as they dove on him they sieved his wings with bullet holes. But he held his course, only occasionally winging away to dodge a diving fighter. Then he saw his leader go. A Zero had passed over Waldron's plane, spraying it with machine-gun fire. Flame shot out from the ruptured gasoline tanks. Waldron, trying to escape the blinding fire, opened the canopy and stood up. At that moment his aircraft crashed, breaking his body and throwing up a plume of water and burning gasoline.

The rest followed in quick succession, and as Gay approached his release point he saw the last plane splash into the sea. *If there is only one plane left to make a final run in, I want that man to go in and get a hit,* had been Waldron's prophetic command. Gay was that man, and the swarms of Zeros diving at him could not bring him down. The carrier in front of him was now turning frantically to starboard, but Gay had it dead-centered in his sights. A few seconds more and he would release his torpedo. Enemy bullets were pinging against the armor of his seat. Suddenly he felt a sharp stab in his left arm as a spent bullet dug into his flesh. He pressed it out with his fingers and then noticed blood on his left hand where a steel fragment had hit him. Then he heard his gunner cry out frantically, "Mr. Gay, I'm hit!"

Gay was upon his target now. The carrier loomed up and he could see men on the flight deck scurrying for cover. The electrical release button was on top of the stick. Gay pressed it, but nothing happened. Quickly he reached over for the manual release cable and gave it a monstrous jerk. Instantly he could feel his plane rise, relieved of its burden.

Gay's wounds, the failure of the electrical release mechanism and the evasive tactics of the carrier all combined to throw his aim off, while Japanese gunners continued firing at him. Tracer bullets converged on his plane. Something shattered on the floor of the cockpit. An explosive shell carried away his left rudder control and burned his leg. The aircraft dipped over crazily and he pulled at the controls to correct the fall. When the plane did not answer Gay knew that he was lost and—after glancing back at the rear-seat-man—alone too. The gunner's eyes were vacant, his mouth open, and his head was tilted over in the angle of death.

Gay's plane wobbled in its flight, soared over the bow of

the carrier, turned south and skimmed for a moment over the waves. He stalled the engine for a crash landing. As he hit, the right wing was torn from the fuselage and went skidding over the water, and he felt the hold-back harness dig into his chest. He pulled at the canopy and water poured into the cockpit. Quickly he swam away, as the Zeros circled overhead. His plane was almost under now, with only the tail section exposed, and soon that sank too, carrying the dead gunner down with it.

Gay inflated his life jacket and swam over to the flotsam bobbing on the sea. He was lucky. A boat bag, containing a rubber raft, had floated free. He tucked the bag under his arm and then gathered in a black cushion which had come loose from the bomber compartment. With this he covered his head to avoid being sighted by the Zeros.[4]

The moment Gay crashed into the sea a Japanese flight leader flashed word to Nagumo that all fifteen of the enemy torpedo planes had been shot down. This was only a brief comfort for Nagumo, for at 9:30 Lindsey's squadron was sighted broad on *Akagi's* starboard bow, coming in low. Lindsey, of course, like Waldron a few minutes before him, had no fighter protection because Gray, for some unexplained reason, was never called to the attack. Furthermore, Lindsey did not even have the element of surprise on his side. Since Waldron's attack, the Japanese carriers were charging about in wide circles, forcing Lindsey to maneuver radically in order to get onto an attack course, and the many Zeros which had butchered Waldron's flight were still at low altitudes, in perfect position to make their strafing runs. But Lindsey and his pilots displayed prodigious fortitude by flying directly into the hail of gunfire. Again the air was filled with diving Zeros and the chatter of machine guns. Lindsey shouted commands while he pushed his rudder over to bring his squadron on a line with the *Kaga*. However, this ship, like all the others of Nagumo's force, was showing its quarter to the attacking planes, forcing Lindsey to make a wide circle in order to get on the carrier's beam. Pursuing this necessity, he exposed himself for several more minutes to the withering passes of Japanese fighter planes. Then his men began to die. There were sudden flashes of fire, a trail of black smoke, the uncontrollable dive, the crushing impact, and the smother of foam settling over the broken aircraft.

Every gun on the screening destroyers that could be brought to bear on Lindsey's flight was firing. Japanese sailors cheered wildly as each plane crashed into the sea. A few pilots dropped their torpedoes blindly, and hopefully, but not one scored a hit. And of these fourteen planes, only four escaped the holocaust and were able to wing away. Lindsey was not among them.

The attack was over before 10 o'clock. Of the twenty-nine torpedo planes that had struck at the Japanese carriers, twenty-five were gone and not a single hit was scored.

From the time Nagumo had turned northward a few minutes after 9 o'clock and set his fleet on a course of 070° to attack the American carriers, he had been closing the range between himself and the *Yorktown*. Meanwhile, since Admiral Fletcher had decided that he could wait no longer to launch his own attack, the first planes of his air strike shuttled off the *Yorktown's* flight deck shortly after 8:30. Massey's twelve torpedo planes were ordered to proceed immediately to the target, while the seventeen dive bombers under Lieutenant Commander Maxwell F. Leslie were instructed to circle overhead for twelve minutes and then proceed to the objective, overtaking Massey's aircraft enroute. Lieutenant Commander Thach's six fighters were not launched until 9:05. This procedure was employed because of the slow speed of the torpedo planes and the limited fuel capacity of the fighters.[5]

At 9:45 the three squadrons rendezvoused, with Massey flying at 1500 feet, two of Thach's fighters 1000 feet above him, and four others at altitudes of five and six thousand feet to shield the low-flying planes from a surprise attack by enemy interceptors. About two miles above these four fighters were Leslie's bombers, winging southwestward.

Since Nagumo had been dodging Waldron and Lindsey with frantic course changes, his formation was widely scattered when *Yorktown's* planes found him about 10 o'clock that morning. Leslie, Thach and Massey had been holding fast to a course which ran left of the one taken earlier by Waldron, and when the Japanese carriers finally were discovered, they were about thirty or forty miles to the north, almost on the starboard beam of the *Yorktown* flight. The three squadrons veered sharply to the right, settled on a course of 345° directly in line with the enemy fleet, and prepared to attack. This was the first air assault which promised to be fully coordinated, with torpedo planes and protecting fighters diving in low and the bombers diving down in from their higher altitudes. But the heavy blanket of clouds which had plagued Gray earlier was to confuse the *Yorktown* strike too. As Leslie flew over the cloud cover he lost contact with the torpedo planes and was unable to communicate with Massey by radio. In the meantime Thach's fighters glided down to cover the torpedo planes and give Massey a fighting chance to steady on an attack course.

As the flight approached the enemy, planes could be seen landing and taking off from the Japanese carriers. Many of the Zero fighters which had been flying over Nagumo's fleet and annihilating the air strikes from both Midway and Task Force Sixteen were now dangerously low on fuel and ammunition. One by one they touched down, were refueled and rearmed, and then took off again, ready to repulse the next attack. There was a jubilation which broke through the deadly tension of battle. Pilots were cheered as they landed, and cheered again as they took off.

Since they had changed the course of their flight, Massey and Thach had covered about half the distance to the enemy fleet when Japanese fighters appeared in droves. Sorely outnumbered, Thach still had time to notice that the Zero pilots were not squandering their superior power in acrobatics, as they had done earlier in the South Pacific. There was no more stunting as they dove in or pulled away from their attacks, and their dives were directed generally from abeam. Diving at high speed, they opened up with shattering blasts of machine-gun fire, went into an almost vertical climb until they began to lose air speed, and then completed a small loop which put them out of reach of the American fighters and in position for another dive.

Thach twisted and turned, gunning his motor and firing

bursts at the Zeros in order to brush them away from Massey. But his planes were no match for the enemy fighters and he soon found himself outclimbed and outmaneuvered. He saw the first of his pilots, bullet-riddled, spiral into the sea.

Meanwhile, as Massey was ordering his squadron to divide into two sections, the Japanese ships began firing. The air was thick with tracer bullets, diving Zeros and splotches of smoke. Falling planes splashed into a sea covered with fuel-soaked flotsam. Thach, who had made famous the two-plane attack known as the "Thach Weave," was able for a few minutes to overcome his operational and numerical inferiority and shoot down several Japanese fighters. But there were too many of them, and one by one Massey's men, caught in the vicious crossfire, wobbled off course, nosed over and crashed. Massey's plane burst into a ball of fire, and before the squadron was on its attack course at about 10:20, there were only five aircraft left. One section attacked the nearest carrier, which was then swinging in a wide circle: the other section veered sharply to the left to engage another carrier farther to the northwest. With Zeros diving at them, these planes made their run ins, released their torpedoes, and immediately winged over to the northeast. Three were shot down as they tried to break clear. None of the torpedoes hit. Once again the sea was littered with the sinking wreckage of shattered aircraft.

The men who had followed Waldron, Lindsey and Massey into battle were brutally bludgeoned. Of the forty-one torpedo aircraft launched from the three American carriers that morning, only six survived—and not a single Japanese ship was hit. Yet the sacrifice was not in vain. These attacks, coming one upon the other in quick succession, had drawn down the enemy fighters from their lofty altitudes, leaving the upper levels clear for the dive bombers which were now arriving.

CHAPTER
7

~~~~~~~~

THE TURNING OF THE TIDE

> . . . each Trojan hoped in his breast,
> that they should fire the ships, and slay
> the heroes of the Achaians. With these
> imaginations they stood to each other,
> and Hector seized the stern of a seafaring
> ship, a fair ship, swift on the brine, that
> had borne Protesilaos to Troia, but
> brought him not back again to his own
> country.   HOMER: Iliad

SINCE HIS departure from the *Yorktown* at 9:02, Leslie, leading his squadron of seventeen dive bombers, had been flying on a course of 225° to 230°, driving hard for the expected point of interception with Nagumo's carriers. If the Japanese were not sighted at this hypothetical position of contact, he was instructed to turn to the right and fly up the last bearing of the enemy reported earlier by search planes from Midway.[1]

Leslie's flight had begun with mishap. His aircraft recently had been equipped with new electrical bomb-release mechanisms. It was the practice for each pilot to arm his bomb after the squadron cleared the carrier and moved into formation. This action would cock the trigger device in the bomb's nose fuse so that it would detonate upon striking its target. When Leslie reached an altitude of 10,000 feet he signalled his squadron to arm bombs, and then leaned over to throw his own electrical arming switch. Either because of faulty wiring or perhaps because of mechanical failure, Leslie's 1000-pound bomb, instead of arming, fell away and dropped harmlessly into the sea.

Feeling his craft suddenly become lighter, Leslie turned in dismay to Lieutenant (j.g.) Paul "Lefty" Holmberg, who was riding in the squadron's Number Two position, just to Leslie's left. Holmberg made signs with his hands to tell Leslie what had happened, and then ordered his gunner to signal the mishap to Leslie's rear-seatman. For a few moments Leslie either could not understand or would not accept the meaning of Holmberg's gestures. Then Ensign Paul Schlegel, flying on Leslie's right side, began to wave his hands frantically, making it painfully clear to the squadron commander that he had lost his bomb.

For Maxwell Leslie this was a bitter twist of fate. He had been in the naval service for twenty years, twelve of which were spent in the air arm of the fleet. He had flown fighters, bombers and scout planes, and at different times during his career had been attached to the carriers *Lexington, Ranger, Enterprise, Saratoga* and *Yorktown*. Since Pearl Harbor he had trained for this moment and had whipped his squadron into a state of splendid war readiness. Now with the supreme test awaiting him, he was entering the battle without a bomb. "When this bad news was confirmed," Holmberg was later to write, "the skipper made many frustrating motions with his hands and lips, as if to say his luck was damnable." Within a few minutes Leslie found out that three other aircraft of his squadron had suffered arming accidents, which meant that he had only thirteen planes with bombs. But at all cost he had to maintain the discipline of the squadron, and he decided to lead the dive anyway and assist in whatever way he could with his fixed machine guns.

He continued to climb until the squadron reached an altitude of 20,000 feet, and it was from this height that he eventually sighted smoke smudges on the horizon to the right of him and correctly assumed that they were from Nagumo's fleet speeding northward toward the American carriers. Immediately he signalled his squadron to wing over to the right to a northwesterly course, and by 10:20 the Japanese ships were only a few miles ahead of him. The mass of clouds which had previously concealed Nagumo were all to the left of Leslie now and he could see a number of large enemy ships starting what appeared to be full-speed evasive turns. Since the Japanese fighters had been busy at low altitudes for almost an hour butchering the torpedo planes, there were none at the upper level where Leslie was. He therefore had plenty of time to pick out his target—a fat carrier almost dead ahead of him.

In the meantime McClusky, having missed the Japanese force at the point of interception because of Nagumo's change of course, continued southward for a little while. Finding nothing in sight, he had decided at about 9:30 to turn to the northward, hoping that Nagumo was to the right of him. His eventual turn *away* from Midway proved to be a masterful stroke of judgment, for it closed the range between himself and the Japanese carriers. However, he was not able to see the smoke which had alerted Leslie because, being to the southwest of *Yorktown's* dive bombers, the cloud cover blocked his view. He might have flown over an empty ocean until his fuel gave out and then, after jettisoning his bombs, made the long glide downward to crash land on the sea. Had this happened, Leslie, with only thirteen effective dive bombers, would have had to face the full power of Nagumo's fleet alone. The planes that rode with Leslie and McClusky represented all that was left of the American air strike.

It had been more than an hour earlier, while Nagumo was driving off the last of Midway's air attacks, that the submarine *Nautilus*, having tried unsuccessfully to torpedo a Japanese battleship, came under a ferocious depth-charge attack by enemy destroyers. While the attack was going on, Nagumo turned his Striking Force away from the area, leaving one destroyer behind to hunt down the American submarine. This lone warship was the *Arashi*, skippered by Commander Yasumasa Watanabe. When after an intensive search Watanabe's sonar operator failed to regain sound contact with the *Nautilus*, he decided to give up the hunt and set course to overtake the rest of the fleet. He was now many miles behind Nagumo and he rang up for FULL SPEED AHEAD. The *Arashi's* bow plowed into the waves.

Watanabe was driving hard on a northeasterly course; McClusky was heading to the northwest. Their course converged and at 9:55, when McClusky glanced down through a break in the clouds, he saw the *Arashi's* white trail. He could tell that she was making high speed and guessed that her captain was doing exactly what, at that crucial moment, he was doing—catching up with the rest of the Japanese force. Quickly he estimated the destroyer's course and put his thirty-seven dive bombers on it. So at 10 o'clock that morning, while Leslie was closing in on the Japanese carriers from one direction, McClusky was closing in from another.

Admiral Yamamoto, mastermind of the whole operation, had stationed himself to the northwest of Midway with a force including three battleships, one light cruiser, a light carrier and nine destroyers. This fleet, had it been in a position to help Nagumo, could have brought an assortment of well over two hundred antiaircraft guns to battle with the American dive bombers. But Yamamoto, acting upon instincts which will forever confound naval analysts, positioned his fleet hundreds of miles to the west of Nagumo and therefore could bring no support to his carrier commander when he needed it most.

Leslie came upon the Japanese carriers just at the moment they were breaking formation to avoid Massey's torpedo planes. The *Akagi,* carrying her bridge island on the port side, had been steaming westward for several minutes at full speed and was now astern of the *Soryu,* whose sister ship *Hiryu* was far to the north and barely visible. The *Kaga,* with her bridge structure on the conventional starboard side, rolled northward and was almost abreast of the *Soryu's* starboard beam. When the dive bombers appeared, *Akagi* made a dash to the south. In the meantime, *Kaga* and

Soryu put their rudders over hard and spun around in a tight clockwise turn.

Leslie had already descended to 14,500 feet and was preparing to attack with the bright morning sun at his back. The *Akagi* was to his distant left, so he studied the two carriers ahead of him, both of which were turning to the south. These radical course changes, besides being evasive, indicated that the enemy carriers were getting ready to launch an air strike, since their bows were now faced into the wind.

The 26,900-ton *Kaga*, even from Leslie's great height, looked huge to him when contrasted with the 10,000-ton *Soryu*. "Our target was one of the biggest damn things that I had ever seen," one of Leslie's officers said later. Using only a slight change of course to the left or right, Leslie could have attacked either carrier, but the *Kaga*, because of her great size, was marked for destruction.

Leslie patted his head, a signal which told his wingmen that he was putting his bombless plane into a dive. From level flight he dove down at a 70° angle, with the wind rushing past his wings at 280 knots. Within seconds Holmberg arched over, a 1000-pound bomb beneath his fuselage. Then came the others. The large carrier was squarely in Leslie's sights. He saw dozens of planes spotted for take-off, and forward there was a large red sun painted on the carrier's flight deck on which he took careful aim. At 10,000 feet he opened fire with his machine guns, peppering the deck and bridge with 50-caliber bullets. At 4000 feet his guns jammed; he pulled out and began to climb. Behind him came Holmberg, who could now see the first flashes of gunfire from the fringe of the *Kaga's* flight deck. His dive was perfect as the red disk on the flight deck loomed in his sights. Shrapnel tore at his plane. At an altitude of 2,500 feet, he pushed the electric bomb-release button and immediately jerked at the manual release lever to make sure that his bomb got away.

There was a tremendous burst of fire near the superstructure. Pieces of the *Kaga's* flight deck whirled in the air; a Zero taking off into the wind was blown into the sea; the bridge was a shambles of twisted metal, shattered glass and bodies. Captain Okada, his uniform torn and burned, lay dead amidst the smoking wreckage of his command post. Then came three more vicious explosions, hurling planes over the side, tearing huge holes in the flight deck and starting fires which spread to the hangar deck below. Screaming sailors ran around aimlessly, trailing flames. Officers shouted orders against the deafening blasts. Gasoline poured from the planes' ruptured fuel tanks, and some of the pilots who had not been lucky enough to escape the first bomb blast were cremated at their controls.

The fire raced along rivulets of gasoline, spreading disaster below decks. Men trapped behind blistering bulkheads were roasted alive. Hoses rolled out in a frantic effort to hold back the flames caught fire. Some officers and men, their uniforms smoldering and their faces blackened by smoke, were driven back to the edge of the flight deck and from there they leaped into the sea. Then the fire traveled to the bomb storage lockers. Suddenly there was a thunderous detonation, and sheets of glowing steel were ripped like so much tin foil from the bowels of the ship. The hangar deck was a purgatory within a few minutes, and great clouds of black smoke rose from the *Kaga*, carrying with them the smell of burning gasoline, paint, wood, rubber and human flesh.

Less than two minutes after Leslie's bombers transformed the *Kaga* into a flaming cauldron, McClusky's squadron was ready to pounce on the *Akagi* and *Soryu*. The destroyer *Arashi* had led the *Enterprise's* dive bombers directly to the Japanese Striking Force. Even before Leslie had winged over into his dive, McClusky was picking out his victims. He saw two carriers just ahead turning into the wind to launch aircraft. Dividing his flight into two sections, he called out targets and then signalled his descent. One flight pushed over toward the *Akagi*, the other toward the *Soryu*. It was 10:26.

The first of McClusky's 1000- and 500-pound bombs whistled toward their targets. One bomb crashed near *Akagi's* after elevator and detonated with a hellish blast in the hangar, where a number of planes were waiting to be lifted to the flight deck. The shock wave exploded torpedo warheads, tearing men to bits and starting dozens of gasoline fires. Damage control parties struggled heroically to isolate the flames, but clouds of hot black smoke enveloped them and one by one the men collapsed from the fumes. Another bomb struck the flight deck, scattering planes and pilots into the sea. Within a few minutes the flagship was a floating pyre.

Because of the inferno, damage reports were slow in coming to the bridge, but the *Akagi's* skipper, Captain Taijiro Aoki, hearing the dull thunder below decks, had no illusions about the fate of his ship; nor did Rear Admiral Ryunosuke Kusaka, Nagumo's Chief of Staff. Both men understood that the bomb hits were fatal and that the *Akagi* was doomed.

Nagumo, however, was unwilling to accept the fact that the tide of battle was shifting with such appalling speed in his disfavor. Aoki politely told him that the ship was finished and would have to be abandoned. Nagumo's anger flared up. The situation *had* to be brought under control; he would not leave the ship. Kusaka, who was well acquainted with Nagumo's fiery temper, tried to intervene as diplomatically as possible.

"Sir, our radio is smashed and we cannot communicate with the other ships. Should you not transfer your command to another vessel so that you can continue to direct the battle?"

Nagumo still refused to abandon ship. Finally Kusaka directed several officers to take the Admiral by the hand and pull him away. By now the fires were swirling around the bridge, blocking their descent by ladder, and they had to make their escape by a line hanging from the bridge structure.

The scene on the flight deck was grotesque: craters belching smoke, twisted wreckage, and the bodies of officers and men scattered everywhere. The unmanned machine guns, heated by the fires, began to spray bullets in all directions. Now and then a dull explosion came from deep inside the ship.

A destroyer came along side the *Akagi* and took the Admiral and his staff to the cruiser *Nagara,* from whose mast Nagumo broke his flag. From her bridge he watched his splendid command disintegrate.

The *Soryu* had been bombed too. Her engines were

stopped, water poured into the bilges, the pumps failed to work, and hundreds of scorched sailors, fleeing before the flames, threw themselves into the sea. *Soryu's* commanding officer, Captain Ryusaku Yanigimoto, stood resolutely on his blackened bridge. A destroyer pulled alongside and an attempt was made to persuade him to leave the doomed ship. He refused to be rescued and was last heard calmly singing the Japanese national anthem, while clouds of smoke closed about him.

All three carriers were fiery derelicts now, and fire fighting parties left on board fought a losing battle against the flames. Many sailors from the *Kaga* were swimming in the oily water when a torpedo from an American submarine streaked toward their burning ship. Instead of exploding it struck the *Kaga's* side at an angle and then came apart, the warhead sinking and the buoyant after section floating free. Immediately several Japanese sailors swam over to the floating part and hung on.

The *Kaga* burned fiercely throughout the entire afternoon and by twilight was a gigantic torch lighting up the evening sky. At 7:25 she was shaken by heavy explosions, and slipped beneath the waves with hundreds of her crew.

Akagi's fire fighters were able to do no better against the searing flames which gutted their ship. At 5:15 that evening Captain Aoki ordered the Emperor's portrait removed. With a solemn ceremony, the picture was unhooked from the bulkhead, carried through an honor guard, and then placed on board a destroyer which carried it away. Two hours later the raging fires had reached the engine rooms, and Aoki ordered his crew to abandon ship. All through the long night she drifted, throwing her flickering light against the black sky. She was still drifting the next day when dawn broke, and she was finally sent to the bottom by a torpedo from a Japanese destroyer, in order to prevent her from being boarded and salvaged by the enemy. She went down about twenty miles to the westnorthwest of *Kaga,* but many of her crew were saved.

The *Soryu,* last to be hit during the morning dive bombing attack, was the first to go. Flames engulfed her, and at 7:13 that evening she rolled under, carrying her captain and over 700 of her crew with her. She went down only twenty-five miles to the northwest of *Kaga.*

Although the three carriers managed to stay afloat for hours the battle had early been decided by Leslie and McClusky. The dive bombing attack had taken place between 10:24 and 10:26, and in those two crucial minutes Nagumo lost seventy-five percent of his carrier force—marking the beginning of the end of Japan's imperial ambitions in the Pacific.

However, even while the three carriers were burning, the Japanese tried to wrest an ultimate victory from defeat. While Nagumo shifted his flag to the *Nagara,* tactical command was assumed temporarily by Rear Admiral Hiroaki Abe, who rode in the cruiser *Tone.* At 10:50 he informed Yamomoto and Kondo, commander of the Midway invasion fleet, that fires were raging aboard the *Akagi, Kaga* and *Soryu,* but that he planned to attack the enemy carriers with the surviving *Hiryu.* This Japanese carrier, because she had beeh so far north when the American dive bombers arrived, was not immediately sighted and therefore enjoyed immunity for another six and a half hours. From her masthead flew the flag of Rear Admiral Tamon Yamaguchi. While several destroyers circled about the three burning carriers, Abe signalled Yamaguchi to launch an air attack against the American ships; Yamaguchi, a forceful and far-sighted individual, had already given the command. At 10:40, just sixteen minutes after Leslie had led his own attack against the *Kaga*, eighteen Japanese dive bombers, under Lieutenant Michio Kobayashi, with a light fighter escort, were taking off from the *Hiryu's* flight deck, and by 11:00 they were speeding northeastward. The bombers climbed to 13,000 feet and took their heading from several American planes which were returning from their recent attack, unwittingly leading the enemy to their carrier.

The American carrier which Admiral Abe decided to attack was the *Yorktown*, for the Japanese scout planes which sighted Task Force Seventeen did not discover Spruance's two carriers. At 11 o'clock that morning, the *Yorktown*, hull down to the northwest, was spotting ten planes for a reconnaissance flight which was to fan out from 280° to 020° (for Fletcher was still convinced that there was a fourth enemy carrier somewhere to the northwest). Following the launching of the search group, the *Yorktown's* hangar deck was spotted with seven aircraft fully gassed and loaded with 1000-pound bombs. Thirteen more were readied on the flight deck for immediate launching, while a dozen fighters rose into the wind to orbit above the *Yorktown's* wake on combat air patrol. These planes had just been launched when two bombers from the *Enterprise* attack group, with tanks almost dry, touched down on the *Yorktown's* flight deck. They had been badly shot up in the action and were immediately

struck below. Then four of *Yorktown's* own fighters landed
with sputtering engines and wobbly wings. Some exhausted
pilots landed on the wrong carriers: but they were the lucky
ones. Many never got back.

While these aircraft were winging homeward, Lieutenant
Michio Kobayashi's eighteen dive bombers and six Zeros
were dropping down to lower altitudes to avoid detection
by enemy lookouts. Precisely at 11:59 the *Yorktown's* radar
officer, Vance M. Bennett, watched a group of phosphores-
cent "pips" moving in from the left on the scope. Their speed
told him that they were returning echoes from approaching planes. For a few seconds he tracked them. They were
forty-six miles away, coming in on a course of 250°, which
would bring them directly to the *Yorktown.* Immediately he
called to the bridge, warning both Admiral Fletcher and
Captain Buckmaster of the impending attack. At that moment there were several fighters being gassed. Refueling
was stopped instantly. On the *Yorktown's* stern there was an
auxiliary fuel tank holding 800 gallons of aviation gasoline.
Buckmaster ordered it dumped over the side. Fuel lines were
drained and then refilled with carbon dioxide gas under
twenty pounds of pressure. Watertight doors were slammed
shut and dogged down, and the fighters which had been
circling over the *Yorktown* were vectored out to meet the
incoming Japanese.

Lieutenant Commander Leslie, who had already led his
dive bombers triumphantly into the carrier's landing circle,
was ordered to form a combat air patrol and to stay clear of
the *Yorktown's* antiaircraft fire. Doctors and pharmacists
mates rushed to the wardroom, where they waited for

wounded shipmates to be carried in; gunners cocked their weapons; and damage control parties, stationed throughout the ship, were poised for the first explosion. On the flag bridge Admiral Fletcher, helmet pushed down over his head, pored over a large chart and plotted his next move, while the officers and men about him buttoned up their shirts to the neck, rolled down their sleeves, and tucked trouser legs into their socks as a precaution against flash burns.

In a few minutes the *Yorktown* was ready for action. Her cruisers and destroyers were maneuvering at 25 knots into an antiaircraft screening formation, 2000 yards away from her. Every gun that could be trained toward the western sky was fixed on the tiny cluster of Kobayashi's planes rising from the distant sea. American fighter pilots, with guns blazing, intercepted the Japanese squadron when it was still twenty miles to the west of the *Yorktown*. Captain Buckmaster, through his binoculars, could see a long trail of black smoke with a bright spot of flame leading it downward to the sea. Then came others as his fighter planes lashed furiously at Kobayashi's bombers.

Marc Mitscher, staring northward from the *Hornet's* bridge, could also see the falling planes. Suddenly he sighted several aircraft heading for his ship and braced himself for an attack; but after a few tense moments they were identified as American dive bombers. They were, in fact, planes from Leslie's flight which, having been waved off from the *Yorktown* because of the Japanese attack, were trying to land on the *Hornet* before all their fuel was gone. Mitscher cleared the deck for them, but one aircraft, flown by a wounded pilot, crash-landed with such force that all its machine guns began firing, spattering the bridge and deck with .50 caliber bullets which killed an admiral's son and four enlisted men and knocked down twenty others to the deck.

Far away on the horizon *Yorktown's* fighters took a heavy toll of Kobayashi's bombers. Eleven plummeted into the sea, and only seven of the original eighteen were able to break through the combat air patrol and the antiaircraft fire from the carrier's screening cruisers and destroyers. As the Japanese planes approached their diving position, Captain Buckmasted had his 5-inch guns firing, his engines turning for their maximum speed of 30.5 knots, and his helmsman shifting the rudder from left to right to throw off the enemy's aim. Then the lead plane arched over to begin its dive.

Everyone dropped instinctively as the first bomb came down, but it missed the *Yorktown,* throwing up a geyser of gray water on the carrier's starboard side.[2] The pilot never pulled out of his dive. After leveling off, he flew close aboard the port side of the ship, thumbing his nose at the *Yorktown's* bridge. A bullet ripped into his tail and he plunged into the sea off the carrier's bow. The second Japanese pilot released his bomb just before his plane drove through a withering antiaircraft crossfire and disintegrated in its flight, part of its wing falling on the *Yorktown's* deck. The bomb crashed on the starboard side of the ship near the Number Two elevator and tore a huge hole in the flight deck. Many of the men who were manning the guns in this area of the ship were killed, and bomb fragments, spattering the deck below, started fires in three stored aircraft. Lieutenant A. C. Emerson, the hangar deck officer, made a desperate lunge for the sprinkler system, releasing a curtain of water which doused the flames.

The next bomb came down in a perfect trajectory, ripped through the flight deck and detonated with a hollow roar deep inside the smoke stack. The sudden flash of heat was intense. Shards of burning paint flaked off the stack; photographic film in the ship's dark room caught fire; flames spread into the Executive Officer's compartment, and the uptakes were ruptured. Clutching the weather screen of the flag bridge, Commander Walter G. Schindler, Fletcher's Gunnery Officer, watched the attack with a British naval observer, Commander Michael B. Laing, who, between bomb drops, jotted down hasty notes.

The third and last bomb to hit the *Yorktown* speared through the starboard side and exploded below decks. The terrific heat generated by the detonation started wild fires in a rag stowage compartment which was alarmingly close to the forward magazines and gasoline tanks. The fuel storage compartment was quickly bathed in carbon dioxide and the magazines flooded. Meanwhile damage control parties tried to smother the burning rags.

This was the extent of Kobayashi's spirited attack. His decimated flight returned to the *Hiryu*, while smoke billowed from the *Yorktown*. The retreating Japanese air strike consisted of only five dive bombers and three fighters, and it was not Kobayashi who led them away, for he had fallen in flames.

The second bomb had stabbed its way into the very bowels of the *Yorktown*. Three uptakes, which carried combustion gases away from the fire rooms, were severely shattered; two boilers were completely disabled, and the fires under three others were snuffed out; and choking, acrid smoke in several of the fire rooms drove personnel up the ladders. The ship's speed dropped abruptly: twenty knots, fifteen, ten, then six.

The officers and men in the Number One boiler room sweated behind their gasmasks. With two burners working, they managed to keep a head of steam in the boiler, restoring to the battered ship a limited amount of her former strength. At 12:20, however, all engines stopped and the *Yorktown* came to a halt.

Admiral Fletcher now faced the same unpleasant necessity which Nagumo had faced less than two hours before when the *Akagi* was hit. The *Yorktown's* radar was crippled, leaving her blind; planes in the air, in need of refueling, were directed to land on the *Enterprise* and *Hornet;* and *Yorktown's* immobility, which transformed her into a sitting duck, rendered her useless as a flagship. It became imperative for Fletcher to transfer his flag to another ship so that he could direct the battle and maintain communications with Admiral Spruance. Reluctantly he signalled Rear Admiral William W. Smith, Cruiser Group Commander riding in the *Astoria*, to take him off the burning carrier, and then he ordered Spruance to send air cover to the *Yorktown*.

While Fletcher rounded up several key people of his staff, the *Astoria's* motor launch was lowered to the water's edge, then bucked through the slight swells, finally positioning itself below the massive gray wall of the carrier's side. Manila lines dangled from the flag bridge to the launch and officers and men began the long seventy-five-foot descent, hand over hand. Admiral Fletcher put a leg over the weather screen, got a grip on the line and then thought better of it. "I'm too damn old for this sort of thing," he said. "Better lower me." A bowline was tied in another line, looped around his waist, and he made the descent to the launch with several sailors paying out the line from the smoking flag bridge. Once on board the *Astoria*, Fletcher said, "Tell the *Portland* to take the *Yorktown* in tow." The *Portland* was another cruiser attached to Task Force Seventeen.

Admiral Spruance, whose *Enterprise* was hull down on the horizon, had sighted the smoke pouring from Fletcher's flagship, and at 12:35 he signalled the cruisers *Pensacola* and *Vincennes*, both of his own screen, plus two of his destroyers to strengthen the *Yorktown's* antiaircraft barrage in case another Japanese air attack developed. And one did.

Before Leslie's and McClusky's bombs fell, Nagumo had ordered a new, fast scout plane to take off from the *Soryu* and shadow the American force. This pilot managed to see things which the pilots of the *Hiryu* attack group had missed. Kobayashi's fliers, after bombing the *Yorktown*, reported enthusiastically by radio that the enemy carrier— the only one the Japanese knew anything about at the time —was smoking and dead in the water. This news, of course, cheered the Japanese admirals, but only temporarily. When the pilot of the *Soryu* scout plane returned from his search mission and found his carrier in flames, he immediately landed on the undamaged *Hiryu*, rushed to the bridge and informed Admiral Yamaguchi that his radio had not been working and he could only now report that the American force was composed not of one carrier but three! [3]

Yamaguchi immediatedly decided to launch another attack, but there were only ten torpedo planes and six fighters ready for immediate take-off. Feeble as this strike was, Yamaguchi could not waste a moment, for he had to cripple the other two American carriers before they crippled him. He ordered the flight launched without delay.

The strike was put under the command of Lieutenant Tomonaga, who had led the attack on Midway earlier that morning. He climbed into his cockpit with Oriental calm, although he must have known that for him this flight had no return. His left wing tank had been shot full of holes over Midway and he roared off the *Hiryu's* flight deck with only his right tank topped off.

At 12:45 Tomonaga's flight was heading eastward while the *Yorktown's* repair parties, with feverish speed, put out the fires, cleared away the charred wreckage and patched up the holes in the flight deck. By 1:40 that afternoon the jagged holes in the exhaust uptakes were closed off and repairs deep inside the ship were well enough along to allow the engineers to cut in four boilers. A coppery haze drifted from the lip of the *Yorktown's* stack. Slowly she began to move; men cheered; the blue and yellow breakdown flag, flying from the foretruck since the attack, was hauled down with a jerk, and then the engine room reported: "We're ready to make twenty knots or better."

Fighters on combat air patrol were called down for refueling, and the ship turned majestically into the wind. Leslie and Holmberg, who had been waved off during the first attack were now signalled to land. Only moments before, their fuel tanks had run dry and they were forced to glide down near the *Astoria,* crashing into the sea. Leslie and his gunner climbed into their rubber raft and were soon picked up by the cruiser's launch. Holmberg, who made a fine water landing despite the fact that one wheel would not retract, stepped out on the wing of his plane with his chart-board and parachute. His gunner dragged out the rubber raft, inflated it, and they both stepped inside just as the plane sank. The raft had been punctured by a piece of shrapnel and within a few minutes both men were treading water. However, the launch arrived quickly, hauled them in and brought them to the *Astoria.*

Fighters had already landed on the *Yorktown* and were being refueled when the ship's radar operator picked up another flight of planes on a bearing of 340°, thirty-three miles away. The alarm clanged throughout the ship, fueling was stopped, guns were manned, and Buckmaster braced himself for another attack. Gasoline lines were again drained and refilled with carbon dioxide; six fighters orbiting overhead were vectored out to meet the incoming attack, and eight of the ten fighters on board, each with a little more than twenty gallons of gasoline in their tanks, began rolling off the flight deck and climbing into the bright northwestern sky.

Tomonaga's air strike was intercepted when it was about ten miles from the *Yorktown.* While the American fighters engaged the Zeros, Tomonaga ordered his torpedo planes to break formation and attack the carrier from different angles. Two or three, spattered with machine-gun bullets, crashed before they could launch their torpedoes; Tomonaga was able to drop his only an instant before his plane took a

direct hit and exploded, scattering pieces of wing and fuselage over the sea. The encircling cruisers and destroyers
looked like a mass of flame as every gun fired at the attackers.

The last *Yorktown* fighter to take off was in the battle before its wheels were cranked up. The pilot banked to the
right, opened fire on a torpedo plane, climbed and was hit
in turn by a diving Zero. With his aircraft out of control he
looped over, bailed out, floated down to the water and was
rescued by a destroyer after he had been in the air only
about sixty seconds.

Of the five enemy planes which survived the attack, four
made fairly accurate torpedo drops. The *Yorktown* twisted
violently and avoided two torpedoes, but the other two
crashed into her port side. There were muffled explosions,
like rolling thunder, and it seemed to those on deck that
the *Yorktown* had been lifted a foot or two out of the water.
Paint flew off the bulkheads, books toppled from their racks,
and electrical power failed, plunging the lower decks into
darkness. The whine of the generators petered out; the rudder, turned to the left at the time of the explosions, was
jammed tight, and the steam pressure which had given the
Yorktown a momentary reprieve vanished.

Men stared at each other; a few looked over the side,
dumbfounded, and saw beneath the yellowish haze of the
explosion a pool of black oil which was pouring from the
Yorktown's ravaged side. The deck was no longer even.
Shortly after the torpedo attack the clinometer showed a
list of seventeen degrees, and this continued to increase until it reached an alarming twenty-six degrees. Chairs in the
officers' wardroom glided along the deck and tumbled in dis-

order against the port bulkhead, and the pots and pans in the galley hung at a rakish angle. It was difficult to walk and many sailors could not get their bearings in the darkness below and bumped into one another as they tried to find a way out of their listing compartments. Up on the flight deck hoses were being run out, and a mess attendant, member of a gun crew, was running around with a 5-inch projectile cradled in his arms.

Commander C. E. Aldrich, the ship's damage control officer, informed Captain Buckmaster that without power for counterflooding he could do nothing to correct the list. Lieutenant Commander J. F. Delaney, the engineering officer, had already reported that all the fire rooms were dead and all power lost. The list had diminished the *Yorktown's* righting moment and the flooding reduced her stability.

The torpedo had plowed into *Yorktown's* side fifteen feet below the waterline, and the concussion wave warped the quick-acting doors on the third deck. Many of the living compartments on the fourth deck were flooded, and gurgling sea water had already reached the first platform level in the forward and after engine rooms. She was heeled over so far to port now that Buckmaster felt she might turn turtle in a few minutes. Wearily he turned to an officer nearby. "Pass the word to abandon ship," he said.

C H A P T E R
8

~~~~~~~~~~

"OCCUPATION OF MIDWAY
IS CANCELLED"

*Xerxes, when he saw the extent of his
loss, began to be afraid lest the Greeks
might be counselled by the Ionians, or
without their advice might determine to
sail straight to the Hellespont and break
down the bridges there. . . .*
HERODOTUS: *Persian Wars*

IMMEDIATELY after Captain Buckmaster ordered the listing
Yorktown abandoned, the wounded were gathered up and
lowered to a small fleet of boats and life rafts, many of which
had been sent alongside the carrier by the accompanying
cruisers and destroyers. Officers and men carried their shipmates from battle dressing stations, from the sick bay, from
flooding engine rooms, and assembled them at different stations of retreat. Those with superficial wounds went hand
over hand down the lines which hung like jungle vines from
the *Yorktown's* hangar deck; the more seriously wounded

were strapped onto stretchers and lowered to the boats.

There were hundreds of men in the water now, struggling to get to the outer fringe of the fuel oil from the *Yorktown's* ruptured side. It clung to them like slime, getting into their eyes and blinding them. Those who swallowed it soon felt nausea. The rescue boats, with several rafts in tow, moved cautiously through clusters of survivors and hauled them aboard. One boat, streaming two life lines, was already loaded to the gunwales with survivors, but men still tried to climb aboard, and once or twice the craft was almost swamped. The boat officer in desperation had to wave a gun in the faces of the struggling sailors in order to get them to take the life lines astern.

When the boats had collected all the men they could carry, they drew away from the oil slick and went alongside the waiting destroyers. There the wounded began their struggle for survival; some died before the overworked doctors could get to them; others, dazed and shivering, lay about the destroyers' decks while pharmacist mates sought out the critical cases. The greatest medical difficulty was the sticky fuel oil, which ordinary soap and water would not wash away; one doctor tried to scrub the black stuff off with carbon tetrachloride. A great many men were peppered with small bomb fragments, and required blood and plasma; a few underwent immediate surgery; almost everyone who had come down the lines suffered from painful rope burns, which left palms raw and bleeding.

From the *Yorktown's* bridge Buckmaster watched the rescue boats moving back and forth. Soon the Executive Officer, Commander Dixie Kiefer, reported that all the wounded personnel had been evacuated and that the rest of the crew was off the ship. Buckmaster then told Kiefer that there was nothing more he could do on board and sent him over the side. In his descent Kiefer fell, striking the *Yorktown's* canted hull, and was fished out of the sea with a broken ankle.

Buckmaster left the bridge, stepping over the disorder of broken glass, charts, navigational books and binoculars. So far as he knew he was alone with his ship's dead. Balancing himself against the carrier's crazy lean, he inspected the starboard side of his ship from the catwalk to the 5-inch gun platforms. Then he pushed through one of the battle dressing stations and on forward to Admiral Fletcher's quarters and finally his own. From there he climbed down the ladder to the hangar deck, where he found only the debris of battle and the bodies of dead crewmen. He hobbled across the deck in search of live personnel but found none.

He could hear the echo of his footsteps breaking against the bulkheads, and the clatter of unseen things rolling down the inclined deck. The port side of the hangar deck was almost in the water. Glancing around, Buckmaster decided there was nothing more for him to do, so he moved aft and worked his way down a line hanging from the ship's stern. Soon the destroyer *Hammann* picked him up and brought him to the *Astoria,* where he reported to Admiral Fletcher.

The *Yorktown* refused to die. With her engines cold, her side torn open and her flight deck aslant, she drifted under the afternoon sun, defying the sea and her Japanese assailant. Because she remained afloat, it has been suggested that Captain Buckmaster was too hasty in abandoning ship. The argument, though, is based on hindsight. His ship was badly damaged and had a serious list; he could not have known whether more watertight bulkheads would crack open suddenly under the tremendous pressure of the sea, or whether entrapped air pockets would keep the carrier afloat. Had she capsized, as it was believed she would, Buckmaster would have lost a frightful gamble, not merely with a stricken ship, but with more than 2000 of her officers and men, most of whom would have drowned needlessly. The *Yorktown's* stubborn stamina was surely a surprise to many as they watched her that afternoon.

The ten search planes which Admiral Fletcher had so wisely launched before noon had been scouring the sea to the northwest. The plane on the lefthand leg of the search had headed out on a course of 280°, almost due west; the one on the right patrolled to the northnorthwest on a course of 020°. The rest of the aircraft were assigned different courses between these extreme edges of the search pattern. They were instructed to fly out to a distance of 200 miles and report the presence of any enemy ships. It was while this flight was in the air that the *Hiryu's* planes had crippled the *Yorktown*. The search pilots, unaware of the fate of their carrier, pushed on to the terminus of their outbound patrol and then, finding the sea empty, winged over to return to the *Yorktown*. At 2:45 in the afternoon Lieutenant Samuel Adams, piloting one of *Yorktown's* search planes, spied a number of ships on a northerly heading. He studied them carefully, recognized them for what they were, and radioed his discovery to his carrier:

1 CV, 2 BB, 3 CA, 4 DD, 31° 15′ N, 179° 05′ W, COURSE 000°, SPEED 15.

The "CV" was the *Hiryu,* the "BB's," "CA's," and "DD's" her battleship, cruiser and destroyer screen; and the position placed the Japanese force a little more than one hundred miles to the northwest of the smoking *Yorktown.* Fletcher, who was now steaming eastward, received the message on the *Astoria's* bridge. It proved that there was a fourth carrier to westward, just as he had surmised, but unfortunately he could do nothing about it since he had no air power. However, Admiral Spruance received the message too, and immediately plotted an attack. Twenty-four dive bombers, many of them refugees from the *Yorktown,* were spotted on the *Enterprise's* flight deck, eleven of them with 1000-pound bombs, thirteen with 500-pounders.

The squadron was under the command of Lieutenant Gallaher, who had struck his first blow earlier that day as a member of McClusky's flight. At 3:30 the first plane lifted off the flight deck and Spruance radioed to Fletcher that he was about to attack the Japanese carrier reported by the *Yorktown* search plane. Then he asked: ·

DO YOU HAVE ANY INSTRUCTIONS FOR ME?

Since Spruance had two carriers intact, Fletcher decided to give him a free hand in the attack.

NONE. WILL CONFORM TO YOUR MOVEMENTS.

About thirty minutes later Mitscher had the *Hornet's* flight deck spotted with sixteen dive bombers, and at 4:03 the first one took off and followed *Enterprise's* air strike into

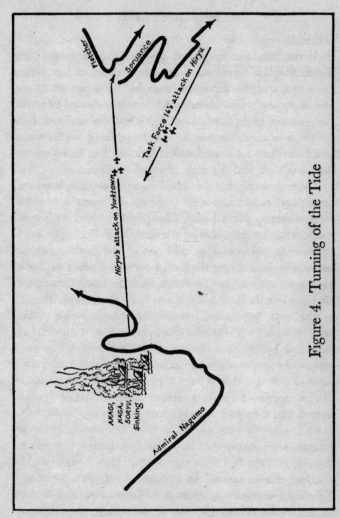

Figure 4. Turning of the Tide

the northwestern sky.

At this time the *Hiryu* was a weary ship. She had been conducting air operations since dawn; many of her planes were lost and the surviving pilots had been driven to the last limits of physical endurance. Her engineers and lookouts, her gunners and plane handlers, her officers and her deck hands were all exhausted by the demands of battle which had been their lot since Admiral Nagumo had launched the air assault on Midway early that morning.

There were only five dive bombers, four torpedo planes and six fighters remaining of *Hiryu's* total air strength of sixty-three aircraft, but Admiral Yamaguchi decided with grim purpose to launch another attack. Misled by faulty intelligence, he believed that only one of the three American carriers remained operative. The surviving pilots of Kobayashi's attack on the *Yorktown* had informed Yamaguchi that the carrier they had hit was *hors de combat*. This, of course, was quite true, but the *Yorktown's* repair parties worked with such stubborn determination after the first attack that by the time Tomonaga arrived with his torpedo planes she was steaming at 20 knots and showed no visible signs of damage, at least from the air. Therefore the survivors of Tomonaga's torpedo attack were understandably convinced that they had scored hits on another carrier, and this error crept into Yamaguchi's tactical radio traffic. First he informed Yamamoto that he planned to destroy the remaining enemy ships in a dusk engagement. How he intended to do this with his meager air strength is not clear. Then at 4 o'clock he sent another message to Yamamoto, advising him of the results obtained by the second attack wave. It read:

"Occupation of Midway Is Cancelled"

TWO CERTAIN TORPEDO HITS ON AN ENTERPRISE CLASS CARRIER (NOT THE SAME ONE AS REPORTED BOMBED.) [1]

The picture of the battle as seen through Japanese eyes at this moment was encouraging. As bad as things had gone up to this point there was, after all, reason for optimism. Only one American carrier, so Yamaguchi believed, was still operable, and this one he planned to attack at twilight. His own depleted air strength would soon receive reinforcements from the converging Japanese forces, for Kakuta's carriers had been directed to speed southward to join him; Yamamoto was driving eastward with his powerful guns and the light carrier *Hosho;* and Admiral Kondo's ships, including the light carrier *Zuiho,* were pushing up hard from the southwest.

However, the Japanese forces were still widely separated. Yamamoto was far to the west. Kakuta, leaving the foggy Aleutians, still had to cover a great distance before he would meet Yamaguchi, and even Kondo, at the time of his decision to help Nagumo, was about four hundred miles away. If Yamaguchi could keep the *Hiryu* (and Japanese hopes) alive through the night and into the next dawn, he might at least expect Kondo's lone carrier, *Zuiho,* to join him. By moving westward he would later meet Yamamoto's eastbound force and pick up the carrier *Hosho.* Then with his air power replenished he could launch an attack against the American force while the other two carriers, *Ryujo* and *Junyo,* were closing in on Spruance's flank. That was at least one possibility. Spruance, of course, was expected to steam into the trap.

Yamaguchi, since he had decided on a dusk attack, used the intervening time to prepare for the strike. Planes were gassed and armed, and the galley served up a rice meal to the *Hiryu's* embattled crew, the first food they had seen since dawn. A token combat air patrol circled overhead and reconnaissance pilots, flying high above the formation, scanned the open sea to the east. It was 5 o'clock.

At 5:01 lookouts on the bridge of the cruiser *Chikuma,* fixing their gaze at the sky high off the *Hiryu's* bow, caught the flash of wings and heard engines. They looked up just in time to see the *Enterprise's* dive bombers overhead. Terrified, they sent out the alarm, but it was too late. Gallaher had come upon the *Hiryu* from the southwest with the afternoon sun at his back, catching the Japanese completely unprepared. The other ships in the screen spotted the aircraft and pumped shells into the air, but Gallaher's planes were already diving. Captain Tomeo Kaku, the *Hiryu's* commanding officer, immediately ordered, "Right full rudder!"

Answering the helm, the *Hiryu* heeled over as her bow curved around to starboard, kicking up clouds of spume. She was in her turn when the first bombs plunged into the sea alongside. At 5:03 she trembled as four bombs in quick succession crashed into her flight deck. The platform of the forward elevator was blasted off its supports and slammed against the island structure; everyone on the bridge was showered with flying glass as the concussion shattered the ports. The yellow haze of the bomb blasts was followed by the black clouds of oil fires. Where the forward flight deck had been there was now a huge crater. One by one the loaded planes caught fire and once again, as in the cases of

Akagi, Kaga and *Soryu*, the flames were fed by spilled gasoline. Bombs and torpedoes blew up in a series of overlapping explosions, hurling wings, propellers, engines and men across the deck and into the sea. Due to careless gasoline storage or to the physical exhaustion of the *Hiryu's* crew—or to a combination of both—the fires very rapidly became uncontrollable. Ladders leading to the engine rooms were enveloped in flames; suffocating smoke rolled through the passageways driving fire fighters above deck; men collapsed from the intense heat; many were trapped deep inside the ship.

While the *Hiryu* burned fiercely, *Hornet's* air strike arrived. Finding the carrier so badly damaged, the pilots attacked a battleship and cruiser instead, but scored no hits.[2] Then came squadrons of Army B-17's flying from Midway and from the island of Molokai, some thirteen hundred miles eastward of the *Hiryu*. These heavy land-based bombers, soaring at great altitudes, were no more fortunate in the late afternoon than they had been in the early morning. Their bombs plummeted into the water, threw up columns of spray, but did no damage to the Japanese force.[3] Later still, Major Benjamin Norris, who had succeeded Major Lofton Henderson as commanding officer of the hard-fighting Marine Scout Bombing Squadron 241, flew from Midway with a force of thirteen bombers to make a night attack on the battered *Hiryu*. This time the squadron did not find the Japanese force and had to return to Midway, guiding itself by the oil fires still burning on the atoll. Only twelve planes returned. Major Norris crashed into the sea.[4]

Meanwhile the captain of the *Hiryu* tried to keep his ship

alive. By using evasive tactics, he attempted to avoid further damage and at the same time escape from the battle area. But the ship's crew fought a losing battle against the blaze. Officers and men in the engine rooms collapsed at their stations. The telephone lines leading to the engineering spaces remained open to the end; Yamaguchi and Kaku, on the smoldering flight deck, were able to receive a minute-by-minute account of the disaster which was taking place in the ship far beneath them, where members of the engineering gang fought the flames with a fatalistic heroism, carrying on until death finally overtook them.[5]

The *Hiryu*, her bilges flooded, listed fifteen degrees. Just before midnight, as destroyers stood by, a group of fire fighters made one last effort to regain possession of the flaming engine rooms, and it appeared momentarily that they might succeed. But then there were more explosions, followed by fresh fires, and it was apparent that the *Hiryu* was beyond saving. The desperate battle had been going on for more than nine hours; more than four hundred men had been killed by explosions and flames; and at 2:30 in the morning of 5 June, Yamaguchi and Kaku accepted the *Hiryu's* fate as well as their own, for according to the inexorable code of the Samurai warrior, one was bound up with the other. Exhausted crewmen were called to assembly to hear Yamaguchi's final words:

"As Commanding Officer of this carrier division, I am fully and solely responsible for the loss of the *Hiryu* and *Soryu*. I shall remain on board to the end. I command all of you to leave the ship and continue your loyal service to His Majesty, the Emperor."[6]

"Occupation of Midway Is Cancelled"

While the destroyer *Kazagumo* came alongside to remove personnel, the assembled crew raised their voices in shouts of "Banzai! Banzai!" The battle flag was lowered, Hirohito's portrait was transferred to a destroyer, and at 3:15, in cool darkness, the first of *Hiryu's* sailors began the long descent to the sea. By 4:30 everyone, except Yamaguchi and Kaku and a handful of men trapped in the engine room, had left the ship. The Admiral and Captain remained on the bridge; the men below—there were thirty-nine of them—had stuck to their battle stations until all engineering equipment had stopped running. Driven into a corner by the smoke, they succeeded in breaking through a deck and getting clear of the fires and wreckage and making their way topside. However, in the encircling darkness they were not discovered by the rescuing destroyers, and so were left behind.

Admiral Yamaguchi, determined that he should not be washed away from the *Hiryu* when she went down, tied himself to the bridge with a piece of cloth. His staff officers pleaded with him to save himself, but he firmly declined. Then Captain Kaku tried to persuade him to leave, but Yamaguchi looked up and said:

"The moon is so bright in the sky!"

Kaku immediately understood that this response carried with it the admiral's final resignation. After a moment Kaku answered:

"We shall watch the moon together." [7]

Both men waved their caps in the air, a farewell to the *Hiryu's* crew. At 5:10 two destroyers fired torpedoes at the listing carrier, ripping her open to the sea. Like her victim *Yorktown*, the *Hiryu* refused to sink, and long after she had been reported scuttled she floated defiantly on. She was even sighted and photographed by a scout plane from Yamamoto's lone carrier, *Hosho,* shortly after dawn, and the men who had broken out of the engine room earlier were seen on *Hiryu's* flight deck. The plane reported the presence of these survivors and efforts were made by other ships to rescue them. But at about 8:15, before help could reach them, the men knew that the *Hiryu* was getting ready for her final plunge. One by one they dove over the side and struck out for an empty lifeboat which, fortunately, was bobbing close by. They clambered on board and from there watched their ship slip deeper into the water. Suddenly she went under, and the men were alone on the open sea.[8]

During the critical hours of the 4th Yamamoto, still several hundred miles to the west, had been receiving a running but somewhat disjointed radio narrative of the battle. Since late that morning he had known that three of his fleet carriers were burning derelicts, for Admiral Abe's 10:50 radio message had conveyed the tragic news, adding that "we are temporarily retiring to the north, and assembling our forces. . . ." the news was confirmed by Nagumo's message of 11:50, announcing that three of his carriers had been bombed, that he had shifted his flag to the cruiser *Nagara,* and finally that he would steam northward after attacking the enemy. At 12:00 Abe sent an amplifying despatch in which he mentioned the "great fires" which were then consuming the *Akagi, Kaga* and *Soryu.* Nagumo had used the word "inoperational" to describe the condition of the three stricken ships. Regardless of what miracle Yamamoto might perform during the balance of the engagement, he would have to accept a seventy-five percent loss of air strength in the vicinity of Midway.

It was apparent that desperate measures were needed, and at 12:20 Yamamoto had begun a grand reshuffling of his forces—the troop transports were retired temporarily to the northwest, while the forces under Yamamoto, Kondo and Kakuta, plus two submarine squadrons patrolling some five hundred miles east of Midway, were directed to attack the American forces. (Admiral Kondo, having listened to the radio news disclosing the fate of the *Akagi, Kaga* and *Soryu*, had already taken the initiative to rush support to Admiral Nagumo.)

Doubtful about the damage done to Midway's airstrips by Tomonaga's dawn strike, Yamamoto demanded decisive action. Kondo was ordered to close the atoll's beaches with some of his heavy guns and bombard the runways; the occupation of Midway and distant Kiska was to be delayed. The substance of these tactical plans, included in Yamamoto's Secret Despatch No. 295, was transmitted from the *Yamato* at precisely ten minutes after one o'clock in the afternoon, just about one hour after Buckmaster had tried vainly to evade *Hiryu's* dive bombers.

Yamamoto's hope for a miracle was contained in his two orders transmitted at 12:20 and 1:10. Yet he knew that Admiral Kakuta, even using flank speed, could not possibly bring his two carriers near the battle area for at least two days or more. The Dutch Harbor feint, since it did not deceive Admiral Nimitz, was proving to be one of the costliest miscalculations in Yamamoto's grand strategy. Neither the

Ryujo nor the *Junyo* had made any substantial gains for the Japanese Imperial Navy in the Pacific, and because these ships were still many hundreds of sea miles away, plunging through damp Aleutian fog, their collective air strength of forty fighters, twenty-one torpedo planes and an equal number of dive bombers could not be used at the crucial moment.

Yamamoto had only a vague and cluttered impression of the enemy forces he was facing. Japanese scout planes, which had been searching eastward with exhaustive determination during the morning and early afternoon, were seeing things that did not exist and missing things that did. It was not until 4:15, during the first dog watch, that Yamamoto received a report which gave him hope, for at that time Yamaguchi radioed:

FROM OUR RETURNING AIRMEN'S REPORTS, THE ENEMY IS APPARENTLY COMPOSED OF 3 CARRIERS, 5 LARGE CRUISERS, AND 15 DESTROYERS. OUR ATTACKS ACCOUNTED FOR 2 CARRIERS DAMAGED.

The "2 carriers damaged" was, of course, the twice attacked *Yorktown,* double-counted by the pilots of Kobayashi's and Tomonaga's air strikes. Yamamoto found the news cheering, almost uplifting. There was hope of Japanese victory at Midway once more. If Kondo could push hard enough, he might be able to bring powerful units of his Second Fleet, and especially the small but now priceless carrier *Zuiho,* into position for a night engagement or, at the very least, a dawn attack. For this to happen, however,

Yamamoto had to hope that the *Hiryu* would remain operable for another day and that Spruance would keep the *Enterprise's* bow pointed westward.

At five minutes to six a defeated and disillusioned Nagumo radioed the following gloomy message to his chief:

BOMBS HIT HIRYU, CAUSING FIRES.

This news should have made it clear to Yamamoto that he had lost his gamble. Nor could he draw solace from subsequent intelligence which told him that the American task forces were steaming *away* from the scene of their recent triumph. Yet, at 7:15 that evening, Yamamoto transmitted an incredible dispatch to his force commanders and even addressed an information copy to the Naval General Staff in Tokyo. His Operational Order No. 158 boldly read:

1. THE ENEMY FLEET, WHICH HAS BEEN PRACTICALLY DESTROYED, IS RETURNING TO THE EAST. 2. COMBINED FLEET UNITS IN THE VICINITY ARE PREPARING TO PURSUE THE REMNANTS AND AT THE SAME TIME TO OCCUPY AF.

He went on to indicate the position, course and speed of his own force, and directed the other forces, less one cruiser division, to "immediately contact and attack the enemy." [9]

Yamamoto's hope was to draw the American ships into a night gun battle, where the enemy's air superiority would be neutralized by darkness. He knew that he would have to work with speed, for if he did not crush the American fleet at night he would expose himself to a dawn air attack. Even if such a carrier-based air strike did not develop, Midway's air strength might have been adequately replenished with aircraft flown in from Hawaii. At 8:30 that evening Yamamoto issued an urgent order to Lieutenant Commander Yahachi Tanabe, skipper of the submarine *I-168* patrolling in the area, to surface and bombard Midway's airstrips until 2 o'clock the next morning. Cruiser Division Seven, under Admiral Kurita, was to carry on the bombardment after that time. Above all, Yamamoto had to depend on the sustained determination of his force commanders, for in such a situation, victory at sea depended as much on brilliant strategy as it did on faith in one's own invincibility.

However, one of Yamamoto's force commanders had reached the end of the line. At 9:30 Nagumo sent a message to Yamamoto which was based upon remarkably faulty intelligence:

THE TOTAL STRENGTH OF THE ENEMY IS 5 CARRIERS, 6 CRUISERS AND 15 DESTROYERS.

Nagumo also advised Yamamoto that this formidable armada was steaming westward and that he was retiring to the northwest, while offering protection to the burning *Hiryu*.

Besides being grossly in error, the dispatch also carried a note of timidity, which made Nagumo look like the weak link in the chain of command. An hour and twenty minutes later he radioed his chief once more, this time specifically referring to Yamamoto's Operational Order No. 158.

"Occupation of Midway Is Cancelled"

THERE STILL EXIST 4 ENEMY CARRIERS . . . 6 CRUISERS AND
16 DESTROYERS. THESE ARE STEAMING WESTWARD. NONE OF
OUR CARRIERS ARE OPERATIONAL. (The understatement of
the war.) WE PLAN TO CONTACT THE ENEMY WITH FLOAT
RECCO PLANES TOMORROW MORNING.

This was too much for Yamamoto, who had lost many of
his weapons but none of his will to fight. Rear Admiral
Matome Ugaki, Yamamoto's Chief of Staff, sneered at
Nagumo's feeble dispatches and said, "The Nagumo Force
has no stomach for a night engagement." [10] Yamamoto
radioed back the following:

COMMANDER-IN-CHIEF SECOND FLEET WILL TAKE COMMAND
OF THE MOBILE FORCE, EXCEPTING THE HIRYU, AKAGI, AND THE
SHIPS ESCORTING THEM.

This meant that Admiral Kondo, flying his flag in the
heavy cruiser *Atago*, was to replace Nagumo, who now had
no responsibility except to protect a couple of burning
derelicts. The *Kaga* and *Soryu* by this time were at the bottom of the Pacific Ocean.

Kondo managed to restore some of the resolve which
Nagumo had lost piece by piece during the long day. Just
before midnight he drafted two dispatches,[11] giving his position, laying down an extensive search plan, and indicating
the time (1 a.m) when he expected to encounter the enemy.
All ships formerly under Nagumo's command, except those
giving aid to the *Akagi* and *Hiryu*, were ordered to reverse

course immediately and participate in the impending night battle.

So it was that during the early hours of 5 June a massive concentration of naval forces, consisting of battleships, cruisers, destroyers and the light but dangerous carriers *Hosho* and *Zuiho,* was moving toward the area north of Midway.

Spruance, meanwhile, after recovering his aircraft from the attack on the *Hiryu,* reversed his course *away* from the converging Japanese ships. He knew that the late afternoon attack on the *Hiryu* gave the American forces, at least for the time being, "incontestable mastery of the air." He did not feel justified in risking a night gun duel possibly with superior enemy forces, but at the same time he did not want to be too far away from Midway at the next dawn. "I wished to have a position," he explained in his battle report, "from which either to follow up retreating enemy forces or to break up a landing attack on Midway. At this time the possibility of the enemy having a fifth CV (aircraft carrier) somewhere in the area, possibly with his Occupation Force or else to the northwestward, still existed."

Consequently Spruance retreated to the east for several hours during the night, turned to the north for about one hour, then to the south, and finally came around once more to the west. These night maneuvers put him out of Yamamoto's reach but made it possible for him to launch an air strike on the Japanese ships early in the morning, of the 5th.

It did not take Yamamoto long to understand what was happening or to realize that he could not hope to overtake the retreating American ships. Just after midnight he drafted an order recalling Admiral Kondo's Invasion Force and the remnants of Nagumo's old command. He followed this with another message which cancelled the scheduled bombardment of Midway and instructed Kurita to join him with his four cruisers, *Kumano, Suzuya, Mikuma* and *Mogami.* Had these powerful cruisers begun their assault, they could have hurled five tons of steel at Midway with each combined broadside. The results probably would have been devastating. But Yamamoto felt that Kurita, because of his great distance from the atoll, would not be able to begin his bombardment until the early morning hours of the 5th. This meant that he would have to expose himself to an American dawn attack from the air and the four cruisers might go the way of the four fleet carriers, a risk Yamamoto was not willing to take.

Defeat was exceedingly bitter for the Japanese. Several staff officers put forth last-minute proposals designed to save face and turn the Japanese disaster into a victory, but Yamamoto, accepting the reality of defeat, refused them. One officer even wondered how they could apologize to the Emperor for the fiasco. To this Yamamoto replied, "I am the only one who must apologize to His Majesty." [12]

At five minutes to three in the morning Yamamoto transmitted this to his fleet:

OCCUPATION OF MIDWAY IS CANCELLED.

He instructed the transports to steam westward out of the range of Midway-based planes, and directed the rest of the fleet to rendezvous the following morning for refueling in position 33° North, 170° East, which is about 700 sea miles to the northwest of the atoll. It was clear he did not intend to come back.

The end had come for Yamamoto, and he knew it far better than some of his hopeful staff officers. To them he said, "Sashi sugi" (enough is enough.) Stomach trouble, which had plagued him earlier, now returned, and he went to bed for a week, asking for nothing more than a bowl of rice gruel to nourish him. There was no medically discernible cause for his illness.

With the cancellation of the Midway operation gloom descended upon the retreating Japanese fleet. There were no more banzais, no more victory songs, no more boast. Yamamoto's yeoman noted that the "members of the Staff, their mouths tight shut, looked at one another. The indescribable emptiness, cheerlessness and chagrin did not bring forth any tears." He observed, too, that in Yamamoto's "ashen face, only his strangely glittering eyes showed his feelings. This exhaustion was definitely not attributable to his stomach trouble alone." Fatigue overwhelmed officers and men alike, and the invasion troops, who had envisaged themselves standing as conquerors on Midway's white sand, could not drink the beer which had been loaded on board their ships for a victory celebration.

Yamamoto's failure to take Midway was bad enough. What made it worse was the fact that this failure resulted in the loss of four fleet carriers with all their planes and most of their pilots. For a nation like Japan, with limited industrial capacities, this was an insupportable loss.

CHAPTER

9

~~~~~~~~~~

THE END OF THE BATTLE

*. . . our citizens can now rejoice that a
momentous victory is in the making.*
FLEET ADMIRAL CHESTER W. NIMITZ

PART OF Admiral Nimitz's defensive strategy was the placing
of a patrol of submarines in the northwestern approaches to
Midway. One of these was the *Tambor*, Lieutenant Commander John W. Murphy, Jr., commanding. During the early
hours of 5 June, while Yamamoto was slowly accepting his
fate, the *Tambor* continued her patrol about 89 miles west
of Midway, on a course of 185°.[1] Murphy, hunched over the
conning tower, chatted quietly with a junior officer, Edward
D. Spruance, only son of Commander Task Force Sixteen.

At 2:15 a.m., just forty minutes before Yamamoto ordered
a general retirement of his fleet, Murphy spied what appeared to be ships moving through the darkness at high
speed. They were, in fact, Admiral Kurita's four heavy
cruisers, steaming away from Midway in accordance with
Yamamoto's Secret Despatch No. 304 transmitted at twenty

minutes after midnight and cancelling the previously scheduled bombardment of the atoll and ordering Kurita to join
him.

Murphy, gliding through a calm sea at 18.5 knots, looked
through his binoculars at the four ships which were about
three miles away on the murky horizon, just off his port bow,
but he could not identify them. It was a difficult situation for
him. He had been forewarned before leaving port that warships under the command of Admirals Fletcher and Spruance
might cross his patrol line during the night. If he should torpedo one of his own ships he would cover himself with
shame. If, on the other hand, he passed up a chance to sink an
enemy warship crossing his bow, his naval career would be
no less damaged.

All he could see was a vague silhouette of ships, and for
two minutes he debated. Then at 2:17 he called an order to
the helm.

"Right standard rudder."

As the submarine moved around to the right, Murphy saw
three more ships to the southwest—the destroyers *Asashio*
and *Arashio*, and possibly the tanker *Nichei Maru*. These he
put astern of the *Tambor* as he steadied on a new course of
030°. At 2:29 he lost contact and quickly pointed the
Tambor's bow due west. For five minutes he strained his eyes
against the black horizon but failed to regain visual contact.

"Left standard rudder," he ordered. "Steady on one eight
zero."

At 2:38 he saw the ships again, coming out of the gloom
to the southwest, but now they were heading northward and
he reversed his own course to parallel theirs. Thirteen min-

utes later the unidentified ships swung about to the north-west and Murphy moved with them. At 2:58 he changed course to 270° to put them in the moonstream, but even then they were indistinct. Suddenly he turned to young Spruance.

"Ed," he said, "if you or anyone else on the bridge can identify those ships as Japanese, I'll shoot!"

Spruance held his binoculars steady for several moments, staring into the darkness. Then he shook his head.

"All I can make out, Captain, are a lot of blobs on the horizon."

Still uncertain of the ships' identity, Murphy continued to maneuver with Kurita's fleet and then sent out a radio report, indicating that he had sighted "many unidentified ships" and giving their position. His report was acknowledged by Midway Radio but he was not advised whether the ships were American or Japanese, a fact which the atoll commanders were in no position to establish. There was nothing for Murphy to do but wait until the first light of dawn, when positive identification could be made. Meantime, he hoped that he would still be within torpedo range if the ships proved to be Japanese. Admiral Spruance had also received the contact report on board the *Enterprise*. From the indicated position he knew that Murphy was not shadowing his task force, but he could not risk breaking radio silence to tell the *Tambor* how things stood.

At 4:12, as dawn approached, Murphy finally recognized the truncated stacks and curved bows peculiar to Japanese warships. Visibility had opened for the enemy, too, and within seconds the closest ship, then only two miles away, veered around toward the *Tambor*, flashing "XJ." Immediately Murphy guessed that this was a challenging signal. He dropped through the hatchway locking the cover after him, and shouted, "Dive, dive, dive." As the *Tambor* disappeared under a welter of foam, he rigged her for a depth-charge attack. Twenty-five minutes later, having failed to pick up any propeller noises, he raised his periscope and found what he accurately described as "two *Mogami* cruisers." They were both headed in a westerly direction and were engaged in frantic signalling with bright, all-directional blinker lights fixed to their foremasts. One was more than four miles away, the other over six.

While trying to maneuver into a favorable attack position, Murphy sent out another contact report. As the sky brightened, he pushed into the gray morning sea with his best speed, only to note with consternation that the range to the enemy was opening. At about 5 o'clock the cruisers were again signalling to each other and maneuvering radically. Murphy noticed that one of them had about forty feet of her bow shorn off. Moments later he heard the muffled sound of distant explosions and this encouraged him to continue the pursuit "with renewed hope." However, at 5:16 the tactical situation had not improved and he knew that he would not be able to overtake the enemy. An hour later both Midway and Pearl Harbor acknowledged receipt of his last contact report. Then at 7:15 he got a message directing all submarines of Task Group 7.1 (Midway Patrol Group) to surface and proceed at their best possible speeds to a position five miles from Midway. Murphy surfaced and headed east, unaware of the damage he had caused to the Japanese fleet.

This is what had happened. As Kurita was speeding toward

the northwest, obeying Yamamoto's command, a lookout on the bridge of the flagship *Kumano* saw the *Tambor's* conning tower in the distance. Instantly he gave the alarm and Kurita ordered an emergency retirement to the left. Turning signals were flashed down the line, but the last ship—the *Mogami*—received the signal late and, instead of putting her helm over simultaneously with the others, plunged across the wake of the *Mikuma*, the ship directly ahead of her.[2] There was a sickening thud, followed by a shower of sparks and the sound of tearing steel. The *Mogami's* knifing bow had driven hard into the *Mikuma's* stern. Damage to the *Mikuma* was not excessive, but the *Mogami* lost a large section of her bow, and while crewmen shored up her forward bulkheads, Captain Akira Soji, her commanding officer, had to reduce speed drastically.

Admiral Kurita sent his two destroyers to escort the damaged cruisers, which were now steaming at about half speed, while he with the *Kumano* and *Suzuya* bent on knots to reach his rendezvous with Yamamoto. The *Mogami* limped along with torn plates curling out into the sea, while her consort left a track of black oil on the water. And that is how things stood when dawn broke.

Yamamoto's order cancelling the Midway bombardment had not been addressed to Tanabe in the *I-168*, stealthily patrolling off the atoll. About forty-five minutes before Murphy had made his first contact with Kurita's retreating cruisers, Tanabe surfaced to begin his bombardment. The gun flashes from his submarine were first sighted by the Marines standing watch at their observation post on Sand Island, and within minutes they returned the fire with their

3-inch batteries. Had this submarine been sunk—or even seriously damaged—during the exchange, the American victory at Midway might have been even more overwhelming than it was. But Tanabe was as cautious in his tactics as he was inaccurate in his marksmanship. The glistening hull of the *I-168* emerged from the darkness in the flickering light of a star shell and the beam of a searchlight. Water spouts kicked up by the Marine gunners were coming uncomfortably close to the submarine; after firing eight rounds, all of which fell harmlessly into the lagoon, Tanabe decided to move away. Thus he saved himself for a grim meeting with the crippled *Yorktown*.

Meanwhile Midway was busy with preparations to stop Yamamoto's retreat. Planes were refueled and armed, and before dawn a flight of Catalinas climbed into the northwestern sky on a search mission, followed by a squadron of Army Flying Fortresses. The *Mikuma* and *Mogami* were sighted by a patrol plane, but the Army bombers, vectored out to the attack, failed to find the reported target.

At 7 o'clock a squadron of dive bombers—six Dauntlesses under Captain Marshall A. Tyler, and six Vindicators under Captain Richard E. Fleming, both Marine pilots—flew off into the morning sky. Because of the deaths of Majors Henderson and Norris the day before, Tyler became the third commanding officer of Marine Scout Bombing Squadron 241.

At 7:45 Tyler and Fleming sighted an oil slick marking the *Mikuma's* trail and followed it. A few minutes after 8 o'clock Tyler spotted the two damaged cruisers. He dove on them from an altitude of 10,000 feet, while Fleming glided down to the targets from 4000 feet. Tyler, coming out of the sun, accounted for a number of near misses, some of which sprayed the *Mogami's* superstructure with jagged bomb fragments and tore holes in her bridge and stack. The *Mikuma* came under Fleming's glide-bombing assault. Although the antiaircraft fire was so intense that he could barely hold his plane in its glide, Fleming brought his obsolete Vindicator to the bomb-release point. At that moment he was hit. Flames tore along the wings of his plane and he finally crashed on the *Mikuma's* after turret. Captain Soji, watching from the bridge, was later to remark:

"The *Mikuma* was not hit by bombs in this attack but I saw a dive-bomber dive into the last turret and start fires. He was very brave." [3]

When the last bomb had been dropped, Tyler led his flight back to Midway. The Japanese cruisers continued on course, with the charred wreckage of Fleming's aircraft riding atop the *Mikuma's* turret.

During the early morning hours of 5 June Admiral Spruance, who had cleverly avoided an engagement with Yamamoto's converging fleet, received *Tambor's* contact report and thought that the Japanese might be moving in for a landing on Midway. He therefore increased speed to 25 knots and set his ships on a course which would bring them to a position somewhat to the north of the atoll.[4] Subsequent contact reports from aircraft seemed to indicate a retirement rather than an assault, and Spruance was able to conclude that the Japanese, because they had lost four fleet carriers and the planes that went with them, were no longer in a particularly offensive frame of mind. Yet he had to hold himself in readiness for an attack, especially since there was still some doubt about the presence of a fifth carrier in the vicinity of Midway.

At about 9 o'clock that morning his advance was delayed when a lookout sighted a ditched American aircraft floating on the water. Spruance ordered the destroyer *Monaghan* to pick up the crew. Two hours later the destroyer signalled that she had overlooked the plane's bombsight, a closely guarded instrument. Spruance sent the *Monaghan* back to recover it, and then ordered her to join the destroyer screen circling around the abandoned *Yorktown*.

Soon the weather began to clear and he decided upon his next move. He had reports on two separate groups of enemy ships; one was to the west of Midway, the other to the northwest. Spruance chose to attack the latter group which, although farther away, contained the crippled carrier *Hiryu* and two battleships, one of them reported as damaged. The "battleships," of course, were the heavy cruisers *Mogami* and *Mikuma*.

Using an aircraft sighting report as a guide, Spruance steamed northwestward at 25 knots, but as the day wore on and there were no further amplifying reports, he began to doubt the reported position of the retreating Japanese force. Still he held to his course, hoping to establish contact with the enemy during the afternoon.

At about 2 o'clock the flight of Flying Fortresses which had left Midway that morning passed overhead. Spruance's routine challenge went unanswered, but he signalled the Army fliers that he planned soon to launch an attack. He heard them report his position and so he knew that Midway was now aware of his westward advance. A little later he heard that the Army bombers had found no enemy ships and were therefore returning to base.

At 3 o'clock that afternoon Spruance turned his carriers into the wind and launched his attack of 58 dive bombers from *Enterprise* and *Hornet*. Although the *Enterprise* planes searched as far as 250 miles to the northwest, and the *Hornet's* 65 miles beyond, neither found the slow-moving cruisers nor *Mikuma's* trail of oil. Three hours later the dive-bomber pilots on their inbound flight made a spirited but fruitless attack on what they thought was a light cruiser or large destroyer. It proved to be the destroyer *Tanikaze*, whose skipper, Commander Motoi Katsumi, had been ordered to determine the fate of the *Hiryu* and had himself already been attacked by Flying Fortresses that afternoon. Katsumi managed to escape the bombs dropped on him and even succeeded in shooting down one *Enterprise* dive bomber formerly attached to the *Yorktown*.

It was already dark when the flights returned and both carriers had to turn on their searchlights to illuminate their flight decks for landings. One *Hornet* aircraft, her tanks empty, splashed just astern of the *Enterprise*, but her crew was quickly picked up by the destroyer *Aylwin*. The attack was an unforeseen waste of bombs, fuel and planes, and it drew heavily on the stamina of the pilots, who felt the fatigue of two days of battle.

That night Spruance pored over his charts again. The weather ahead was not good, but he decided to continue closing with the enemy and so set his force on a course of 280°. However, he slowed his night speed to 15 knots in order to avoid running into a Japanese battleship in the dark, and because he needed to conserve fuel in his screening destroyers.

At dawn on the 6th, Spruance sent off a reconnaissance flight which finally found the crippled enemy cruisers. An air strike of 26 dive bombers with fighter protection was flown off the *Hornet* just before 8 o'clock. Then at 10:45 the *Enterprise's* attack group—31 dive bombers, 3 torpedo planes and a dozen fighters—took to the air. At 1:30, after both attack waves returned with jubilant reports, the *Hornet* launched 24 more dive bombers, the last air strike in the battle.

The first wave hit both ships, but the *Mogami* got the worst of it. One bomb tore through the armor of a gun turret and killed everyone inside, while a second bomb, crashing amidships, wrecked the torpedo tubes and started fires below decks. In the second attack the *Mikuma* took two crushing blows, one forward of the bridge, the other amidships. Flames shot out of ports and hatchways, and the destroyer *Arashio*, trying to come alongside to take off personnel, was driven back by the intense heat and finally had to lower boats to rescue the men who were leaping into the sea. The third wave of planes swooped down on the battered cruiser. One bomb exploded below the *Mogami's* main deck, killing fire fighters and trapping the engine-room personnel. More bombs fell squarely on the *Mikuma*, detonating antiaircraft shells and torpedoes, and the ship began to settle. Groups of her oil-soaked survivors were then standing on the *Arashio's* stern when another bomb fell in their midst and blew them to bits.

Mogami's damage control parties worked desperately to

keep her afloat as the last of the dive bombers pulled away. Their devotion was rewarded. Despite the extreme damage, the *Mogami* stayed afloat and eventually managed to reach the island of Truk. But a year would pass before she was ready for sea again.

The *Mikuma* was not so lucky. Water flooded her bilges, smoke poured from holes in her deck, and she soon took on a severe list which made it clear to everyone on board that she could not survive. While she sank deeper into the sea, the *Mogami* and the escorting destroyers, all of them loaded with survivors, steamed away. About an hour-and-a-half later the *Mikuma* rolled over and disappeared, carrying many of her crew to the bottom. Nineteen men, who were in the water, managed to climb onto an abandoned raft. Three days later the submarine *Trout* found the raft, but there were only two men left; the rest had died of wounds or had fallen into the sea during sleep. One of the survivors was hospitalized for crushed ribs, the other told interrogating officers at Pearl Harbor of the fate of their ship.

There was one other American attack on the 6th. The Army's Flying Fortresses, accustomed to an entirely different kind of warfare, so far had scored no hits. A flight of these giant bombers, which had been sent out to attack the retreating Japanese fleet, failed to locate it and returned to Midway by separate routes. During the afternoon, one group of six bombers sighted what was described as an enemy "cruiser." They flew over the target, releasing a pulverizing load of twenty half-ton bombs. The pilots reported that the "cruiser" sank in the incredible time of fifteen seconds. Lieutenant Commander E. Olsen, skipper of the "cruiser," alias the United States submarine *Grayling* patrolling several hundred miles off Midway, crash-dived his boat before the Flying Fortresses could drop another load of bombs on him. Fortunately he escaped with nothing more than a good shaking up.

After Task Force Sixteen's last attack on Kurita's cruisers, Admiral Spruance, seeking graphic evidence of the damage his aircraft had inflicted, sent out two photographic planes. Previous contact reports had convinced him that his attacks had been launched against a battleship, but when the planes returned and the photographs were developed, he had to reevaluate his damage to the enemy.

It was a time of decision for Spruance. His fliers, after three days of aerial warfare, were exhausted. With their battle efficiency reduced, it would be dangerous to sap their strength any further. Furthermore, his pursuit of Yamamoto's forces had brought Spruance far to the northwest of Midway, beyond the farthest advance of the Japanese fleet. He was, therefore, cruising in waters only recently dominated by the enemy and he had to assume that there would be a number of enemy submarines waiting for him, especially since several had been reported in the area. Besides, if Yamamoto was indeed running away, as various aircraft sightings strongly indicated, there was only the slimmest chance that Spruance could overtake him. Most important of all was the fact that his ships were running desperately low on fuel. At about noon on the 6th the fuel reports of two of his destroyers, *Maury* and *Worden,* were so alarming that he sent them back to fill their tanks from the oiler *Cimarron.* This left him with only four escorting destroyers, below which number he did not consider it advisable to continue. Later in the day, knowing that his force had finally reached the limit of its endurance, Spruance turned his fleet around and moved away from the enemy.

Yamamoto had accepted defeat but he was not yet in full retreat. News of the air strikes on Kurita's cruisers told him that he was being pursued. While the pilots from the *Enterprise* and *Hornet* were attacking the *Mikuma* and *Mogami*, Yamamoto sent the *Suzuya*, *Kumano*, *Atago*, *Chokai*, *Tone* and *Chikuma*, all heavy cruisers, and the light cruiser *Jintsu* with eight destroyers, to the south to rendezvous with the *Mogami*, in case Spruance was rash enough to continue his westward advance across the Pacific. He himself moved to the south, hoping that Spruance might foolishly come within range of Japanese bombers waiting on the airstrips of Wake Island. These wishful preparations simply burned up Yamamoto's precious fuel, for Spruance was already moving away. On the 7th the Japanese admiral finally dispersed his fleet. Some ships were sent to Truk, others went back to Japan, and the transports, loaded with cheerless troops, made their way to Saipan and Guam.

However, the enemy struck a final blow.

Shortly after the *Yorktown* was abandoned, Admiral Fletcher, riding in the cruiser *Astoria*, sent the following message to Captain Gilbert C. Hoover, Commander Destroyer Squadron Two:

DIRECT HUGHES STANDBY YORKTOWN. DO NOT PERMIT ANYONE TO BOARD HER. SINK HER IF NECESSARY TO PREVENT CAPTURE OR IF SERIOUS FIRE DEVELOPS.

The destroyer *Hughes* changed course, headed for the wounded carrier and guarded her during the night of 4–5

June. The next morning the *Hughes's* skipper, Lieutenant Commander Donald J. Ramsey, noted that the *Yorktown* seemed to be no worse than when he had found her the previous evening. He concluded that she might be salvaged and so informed Admiral Nimitz at Pearl Harbor, who was quick to order the fleet tug *Navajo*, the minesweeper *Vireo* and the destroyer *Gwin* to the *Yorktown's* assistance.

The morning silence was suddenly broken by the chatter of a machine gun and the splash of bullets alongside the carrier, and a man was seen on the *Yorktown's* tilting deck, waving his arms wildly. Immediately Ramsey lowered a boat with a boarding party, and two badly wounded sailors, having been left for dead during the abandonment, were taken off the carrier. A search was made below decks for other men still alive, but none were found. Instead, the inspection party discovered several cryptographic devices still on board and a number of classified publications strewn about the deck. The consequences might have been indeed grave had this coding equipment fallen into enemy hands. Such carelessness, suggests that the *Yorktown's* alarming list understandably frightened some people into forgetting their "abandon ship" duties. Every warship carries weighted bags for the disposal of secret publications and precise instructions for the thorough destruction of coding devices. Some cryptographic material was gathered together and sent to the *Hughes;* the rest was locked securely in the *Yorktown's* safes, where it remained while salvage operations got underway.

By noon the small minesweeper *Vireo*, which had been patrolling just east of Midway, arrived on the scene and passed a towline to the *Yorktown*. In the afternoon the *Gwin*, enroute to join Task Force Sixteen before being diverted, hove into view and soon sent a salvage party to the carrier to join the one from the *Hughes*. To lighten the ship, anchors and other movable equipment were dropped over the side, but before much progress could be made night came on and salvage work was halted.

While these preliminary efforts were going on, Admiral Fletcher was busy transferring the *Yorktown's* oil-soaked survivors from the overcrowded destroyers to the cruisers, where there was more room and far better medical facilities to treat the wounded. Finally, after conferring with Buckmaster, he decided to organize a large salvage party and attempt to bring the *Yorktown* into port. Immediately Buckmaster, anxious to save his ship now that he realized she was not going to capsize, called for salvage volunteers and from among them selected 29 officers and 141 enlisted men.[5] With these he boarded the destroyer *Hammann* and set course for the *Yorktown*, taking along the destroyers *Balch* and *Benham*.

By the time *Hammann* came alongside the *Yorktown* at daybreak of the 6th, Buckmaster had already drafted a detailed plan of action. One group of men was to tour below decks to determine how badly the ship was damaged, and then attempt to reduce the list by pumping, counter-flooding and jettisoning everything movable on the port side. Another group was to push all aircraft into the sea. To repel any unexpected air attacks, a gunnery group was instructed to put all antiaircraft guns in working order, and then cut away the heavier guns and topple them overboard. Cooks were to prepare meals for the salvage party, and a medical group was ordered to assemble and identify the dead. These were to be buried after Buckmaster had conducted funeral services.

Several submersible pumps, run by electrical power from the *Hammann*, were lowered inside the *Yorktown* to drain the flooded engine rooms, and *Hammann* supplied a stream of water to fight a persistent fire in the rag stowage compartment. She also kept her coffee urns boiling.

By the middle of the afternoon one 5-inch gun had been dumped overboard and another made ready for dropping; the rag fire was out; two starboard fuel tanks were filled with water as a counter-flooding measure, and considerable progress had been made in pumping out the engine rooms. The *Yorktown's* clinometer showed that she had righted herself by a small but encouraging 2 degrees. Five destroyers [6] circled around the carrier, their sonar gear operating to pick up the returning echo of a hostile submarine. And while the small *Vireo*, with a catenarian cable binding her to the *Yorktown*, was heroically pulling the carrier eastward at a barely perceptible speed, the big tug *Navajo* had long since left her patrol station south of French Frigate Shoals and was racing to the northwest to assist.

Meanwhile, although four Japanese carriers had been destroyed on the 4th, enemy air reconnaissance had not been idle. Just before 7 o'clock on the morning of the 5th, a float plane from the cruiser *Chikuma* had radioed the following message to the retiring Japanese forces:

SIGHT AN ENEMY YORKTOWN CLASS CARRIER LISTING TO STAR-
BOARD (sic) AND DRIFTING IN POSITION BEARING 111°, DISTANCE

The End of the Battle

Commander Tanabe of the *I-168*, who had demonstrated unenviable markmanship during the previous night's brief bombardment at Midway, was now called upon by Yamamoto to take aim on the listing *Yorktown*, which was about 160 miles to the north of him.

On the following day, after a long and frustrating search, Tanabe finally found his target. Raising his periscope cautiously, he took a long time to study his approach and note the maneuvering pattern of the circling destroyers. Slowly he moved to within less than a mile of the *Yorktown*, which meant that some of the destroyers must have passed directly over Tanabe as he moved in for the kill. Perhaps it was due to the thermal gradient, or the turbulence of the destroyers' wakes, or because there was flotsam and oil on the water—or a combination of all these things—but none of the sonar operators detected the *I-168* as it glided deep beneath the destroyer screen. Tanabe, who could hardly miss at this range, took careful aim and shouted, "Fire!" Four torpedoes shot from their tubes, trailing the telltale white tracks. Immediately the cry went up, "Torpedoes!" and gunners on the *Hammann* opened a steady stream of 20-mm fire at the white streaks, but to no avail. One torpedo went wide of the mark, another crashed into the *Hammann*, which was still alongside the carrier, and the other two bubbled beneath the destroyer and dug deep into the *Yorktown's* starboard side with heavy explosions.

Tanabe raced away but soon came under a crushing depth-charge attack by three destroyers which knocked paint off the submarine's bulkhead, put out her lights and released poisonous gases. Once he surfaced, but was driven below again by gunfire. Eventually, with clever maneuvering, he evaded his attackers, and after the sun had set he finally surfaced. He was the only Japanese naval officer to achieve any real distinction in the Battle of Midway.[8]

At first the *Yorktown* did not seem to be badly damaged, although the *Hammann* was. The torpedo had caught the destroyer in the Number Two fire room, opening a large hole to the sea. Tons of water cascaded into the engineering spaces and tore away the forward bulkhead, and the blast of the torpedoes which had struck the *Yorktown* drove the *Hammann* outward, parting all hoses, cables and mooring lines. The shock of the explosions threw the ship's skipper, Commander Arnold E. True, hard against the desk in the pilot house, cutting off his breath and breaking one of his ribs. The Executive Officer, noting how quickly the *Hammann* was sinking, passed the word to abandon ship. A few moments later True got his wind back and was able to hobble to the starboard wing of the bridge. He saw that part of the main deck was already awash, and the sag amidships told him that his ship's back was broken.

By now the stern was riding high. A torpedoman, Berlyn Kimbrell, calmly pulled his way along the racks of depth charges to make sure they were all set on "safe" so that they would not detonate beneath the swimming survivors when the ship went down. Finding several men stunned by the shock of the explosions, he got them life jackets and helped them over the side, and then dove clear himself. Life rafts had been released and men were swimming to them. True made a search of the bridge area for injured personnel. Finding none and seeing the forward decks abandoned, he moved to the forecastle, which was almost underwater, and jumped free.

Less than five minutes had passed since the attack, but already the *Hammann's* bow was under water; a moment later she went down, carrying with her a torpedo that had been activated by the blasts and was spinning hot in its tube. Everyone swam desperately through the oil slick to get away from the suction. Kimbrell was killed by a heavy underwater explosion which came from either an overlooked depth charge or one of the ship's torpedoes.[9] The splitting concussion wave also killed outright a great many of the swimming survivors, and injured about eighty more. Some of these, pulled out of the water by the *Benham*, sustained severe diaphragmatic wounds, and died quickly.

The rescue boats overlooked Commander True and he floated in the oil slick for about four hours. When the *Balch* found him he was almost unconscious. Dazed and in pain, he had been supporting two sailors, unaware that both of them were already dead.

Meanwhile the *Vireo* cut the towline and took Buckmaster and his salvage party off the *Yorktown* and brought them to the *Benham;* before he left the minesweeper, Buckmaster was called upon to conduct a funeral service for two officers and one enlisted man of *Hammann's* crew, whose bodies had just been lifted out of the sea.

As for the *Yorktown*, the two torpedoes which hit her at the turn of the bilge sent up a rumbling shock from keel to masthead. An auxiliary elevator was carried away, rivets in the foremast snapped off, the landing gear of two planes collapsed, and all the identification and personal belongings of the dead, which had been placed in piles on the hangar deck, fell into the sea. Because the *Yorktown* had been hit on the starboard side, her list, strangely enough, decreased to 17 degrees, but the advantage gained by the loss of heeling was more than offset by the fact that she was now deeper in the water. Yet if certain compartments remained water-tight, there was still hope for her. Buckmaster did not intend to give up without a fight, and so he planned to resume salvage work on the following morning, at which time the *Navajo* was expected to arrive.

For several hours the *Yorktown* drifted aimlessly over the darkening ocean, encircled by her destroyer screen. All this time the sea had been pouring into her compartments. During the night she suddenly lunged over crazily to port, and by first light Buckmaster knew that she was beyond hope. When the sun rose she was deep in the water. The destroyers hauled their colors to half mast, and everyone who could stand was at attention, hat in hand, waiting for her to sink. Slowly the *Yorktown* rolled over and all the loose gear on her decks—safes, boxes, tools, chairs, radios, pots and pans—tumbled against the port bulkheads, sending a heart-sickening noise across the water to the silent destroyers. Her flight deck rolled under, then her island, and she disappeared, leaving a coating of oil-flecked foam. Some men wept, all were stunned by the death of this great ship, and suddenly the Battle of Midway became history.

The cruisers and destroyers set course for Pearl Harbor with *Yorktown's* and *Hammann's* survivors. Presently men began to die from their wounds and were buried at sea, while patrol planes from Midway, searching for downed pilots, gathered in the living.

The first news of the battle was cautiously presented by both sides—by Nimitz because he had not yet had time to evaluate results fully, by Yamamoto because he had. But before long newspapermen, combining fact and fiction, gave to the public a distorted picture of what had happened at Midway. The respectable *New York Times* ran a banner headline: ARMY FLIERS BLASTED TWO FLEETS OFF MIDWAY. One California paper published a sensational story related by an Army Air Corps Lieutenant Colonel, telling . . . *How His Squadron Smashed Japan's Invasion Attempt.* Radio broadcasts and newspaper articles extolled the role supposedly played by the B-17's in the battle, and most of the nation believed it. One paper pointed out to its readers that Midway showed what land-based air power could do to naval and air power attacking from the sea, and military people of responsibility exhumed the lopsided "air power" concept which had gotten so much publicity during the 1920's.

It would be inexcusable for a writer, even a naval-minded one, to imply that the Army pilots who flew at Midway were not deserving of praise. True, they did not hit anything, while the naval aviators who wrought the crushing damage on Yamamoto's fleet never got the full measure of credit they so justly deserved. Yet those Army fliers who lifted their great bombers off Midway's airstrip and flew them westward over the open sea were among the bravest, for they also exposed themselves to death, and a few of them did not come back.[10] Those who triumphantly claimed hits on enemy ships sincerely believed what they reported. What caused their excessive claims was the fact that they bombed fast zigzagging targets from great heights from which it was virtually impossible to tell a near miss from a solid hit. High-level bombing was to play a vital part in the war and it contributed vastly to America's ultimate victory in Europe, but it was a technique of little value in naval warfare.

Unlike the extravagant boasts coming from other quarters, Admiral Nimitz's communiqué, issued at Pearl Harbor just as the battle drew to its close, paid tribute to everyone who helped drive back the invaders. "Through the skill and devotion of their armed forces of all branches in the Midway area," he said, "our citizens can now rejoice that a momentous victory is in the making." Then he punned: "Perhaps we will be forgiven if we claim we are about midway to our objective." For him only a battle was over; the war was far from won.

Meanwhile Tokyo Rose, whose mellow voice filled the air waves, was busy broadcasting news of a great Japanese victory at sea. However, this sham was too painful for sensitive Japanese war lords to bear, and soon news channels in Japan were shut off. Midway had become a bitter word. Columbia, N.B.C. and United Press listening posts soon noted that the Tokyo radio was strangely silent on news of the naval battle.

Admiral Fletcher returned to sea after Midway and was again a task force commander two months later, during the Guadalcanal-Tulagi landings and the battle of the Eastern Solomons. During the last months of the war he was still at sea, bombarding Paramushira in the Kuriles. In 1947 he retired and returned, a full admiral, to his Maryland home.

Admiral Spruance became Nimitz's Chief of Staff. Later he went to sea, commanded the Fifth Fleet and led the Gilbert Islands occupation, the invasion of the Marshalls, and the capture of Saipan, Guam and Tinian. His flag was still flying during the battle of the Philippine Sea and the capture of Iwo Jima and Okinawa. In 1948 he retired as a full admiral, but in 1952 President Truman named him as ambassador to the Republic of the Philippines, a post he held until 1955.

Yamamoto did not see the end of the war. He was shot down while inspecting bases in the Solomons. Our cryptanalysts intercepted and decoded the message which described the course of his flight, and he was ambushed in the air. His body was solemnly cremated and the ashes returned to Japan.

The *Hornet,* five months after Midway, went down in the battle of Santa Cruz Island with all her colors flying. The *Enterprise* was lucky enough to see the end of the war, but finally came to an ignoble end. Although she had fought through almost every major battle of the Pacific war—thus symbolizing victory for the nation she served—and although Fleet Admiral Halsey tried hard to raise money to preserve her as a national monument, she was sold for scrap to a New Jersey shipyard.

Midway did not end the war. Savo Island was yet to come, and Cape Espérance and Santa Cruz and Tassafaronga and Leyte Gulf. But it was Midway which profoundly altered the stream of Japanese history.

The climax had passed.

APPENDIX
A

~~~~~~~~~

THE FLIGHTS OF
WALDRON AND GRAY

EXISTING versions of the Battle of Midway describe Task Force Sixteen as launching its planes for about one hour, beginning a few minutes after 7 o'clock. At 8:04, according to *Enterprise's* Air Attack Group Track Chart,[1] all planes were in the air, flying on a southwesterly course. This course was expected to bring the aircraft to a point of interception with Admiral Nagumo, since it was believed he was still moving toward Midway on a southeasterly heading, as indeed he had been doing since 3 June. But because he changed his heading to 070° in order to attack the American carriers, none of the flights from Task Force Sixteen found him where he was expected to be. Accordingly, *Hornet's* bombers and fighters, missing the target, turned south toward Midway and never joined the fight at all.

The *Hornet's* torpedo planes (Waldron), with *Enterprise's* fighters (Gray) overhead, are described as flying on a course similar to the one taken by *Hornet's* bombers and fighters. They turned to the northeast after failing to find the Japanese at their expected position, and later, after sighting smoke, turned northward. The subsequent attack of the torpedo planes ended in disaster. Gray, who had been flying above these torpedo planes, lost them in the clouds before Waldron launched his attack. He then orbited high above the Japanese carriers, waiting for Lindsey (*Enterprise's* Torpedo Squadron) to signal him for support, as had been agreed upon. However, Lindsey, after passing the expected point of interception, so the present version goes, veered sharply to the right, found Nagumo and was struck down by Japanese fighters. Since Lindsey's signal never reached Gray, he remained aloft and did not get into the fight. Meanwhile, *Enterprise's* bombers flew far beyond the interception point, then turned to the northwest, later to the northeast, and finally found the enemy carriers and attacked them.

A possible discrepancy in this version has to do with the outbound flights of Waldron and Gray. How was it possible, one may ask, for Waldron's planes, slow-moving, torpedo-laden, and among the last to be launched, to be the very first American carrier-based aircraft to attack the enemy? At the time of launching, Nagumo's force was estimated to be 155 miles away, bearing 239° from Task Force Sixteen.[2] According to *Enterprise's* Track Chart, the Japanese carriers at the time of the first attack were between 140 and 150 miles away from Task Force Sixteen's launching position. If Waldron left the *Hornet* at 8:04 that morning and began his attack at 9:28, he travelled for one hour and twenty-four minutes. With an air speed of 100 knots,[3] which could not be augmented by the southerly breeze, he would have had to cover no more than 140 sea miles in his flight. Therefore it would seem indisputable that he flew a direct route to the Japanese force with little change of course, for one hour and twenty-four minutes times 100 knots equals 140 miles.

The Japanese log [4] reports the sighting of low-flying planes at 9:18 on a bearing of 066°, distance 10.9 miles (20,000 meters.) This bearing, plotted from Nagumo's position, leads directly to Task Force Sixteen's position, and indicates that Waldron's course, if he were flying on a reciprocal bearing, would have been 246°, considerably to the right of the course followed by the other aircraft. This, of course, assumes that the bearing is true. If we assume it to be relative and apply it to Nagumo's course of 070°, then Waldron's attack course would have been 136° and the hypothesis of a direct flight would be invalidated. However, had Waldron made a sharp change of course after failing to find the enemy carriers at the expected point of interception, he would have added 40 more miles to his flying distance and consequently, taking into account his sluggish air speed and unfavorable wind, could not have attacked before 9:48. We know, though, that he attacked at 9:28 and therefore would have had to fly directly to the enemy.

Furthermore, George Gay, the only survivor of Waldron's lost squadron, has asserted that the flight was direct and that Waldron himself said that he believed the Japanese would change course. This information was given to writer Sidney L. James shortly after the battle,[5] and Gay repeated essentially the same version in 1948 to writer Lloyd Wendt, who prepared a series of nine articles on Torpedo Squadron

Eight.[6]

James S. Gray, who led *Enterprise's* fighters (and who at the time of this writing holds the rank of Captain and commands the *U.S.S. Mount Suribachi*), assured me personally and confirmed in subsequent correspondence that Waldron "headed for the Japanese Fleet in a beeline." He also advised that Lindsey's squadron diverged somewhat from Waldron's, but from his altitude the divergence did not seem excessive. As a general practice torpedo planes used to "spread out," and this, in the case of Waldron and Lindsey, put them a considerable distance behind Gray's fighters. For this reason he "gave up trying to stay over both outfits after launch—having 'S' turned in sight of both during the first ten minutes or so." This information, supported by a track chart on which Captain Gray drafted the course of the flights in question, is of recent date. Nevertheless, it agrees with his own Action Report, written immediately after the battle, in which he says that he rendezvoused over the torpedo planes and flew directly to the target.

Gray circled over the Japanese Fleet on the up-sun side, waiting for Lindsey's prearranged call for help, which never came. He was not able to tell from his altitude of some 20,000 feet what was happening below him. Also, he had expected the torpedo planes to use the low-hanging cloud cover as a shield, as was done in the Coral Sea engagement. "I later learned," he wrote in his report, "that the torpedo squadron made no attempt to use the cloud cover and was ambushed about two miles from . . . (its) . . . objective." [7]

Since Gray had lost sight of the low-flying torpedo planes,

he tried to make visual contact with his own dive bombers in order to cover them at their push-over point. But these, of course, sweeping around the Japanese force in a clockwise manner, did not come upon Nagumo's wake until almost 10 o'clock, and consequently were not seen by Gray. Because he carried no bombs, Gray considered making a strafing run on the Japanese ships but decided against this since his fighter planes, loaded down with "store bought" armor in the form of boiler plates, were running dangerously low on fuel. His decision kept the *Enterprise's* fighters out of the initial phase of the battle but enabled them to pursue the enemy during the remainder of the long encounter. For his later strafing attacks on enemy ships, which he carried out "with fortitude and calm perseverance . . . in the face of concentrated anti-aircraft fire and determined fighter opposition," so the citation reads, Gray was awarded a Gold Star in lieu of a second Distinguished Flying Cross.

Gray's observation that the divergence in course between Waldron's and Lindsey's squadrons "did not seem excessive" explains to some extent how *Enterprise's* torpedo planes were able to sight the Japanese carriers only two minutes or so after Waldron began his attack.[8] It would seem that Lindsey had split the angle between Waldron's direct course and that of the rest of Task Force Sixteen's aircraft, thus putting himself within visual distance of Nagumo's northbound fleet at 9:30 and making it possible for him to attack about ten minutes later. Lindsey's attack was more prolonged than Waldron's because the enemy's violent evasive maneuvers forced him to waste valuable minutes circling around to get on a good attack course.

It is apparent that the confusion attending the first air strike—the torpedo planes attacking without fighter cover; Gray's orbiting over the enemy fleet, waiting for the call that never came; McClusky's missing Nagumo at the anticipated point of contact; *Hornet's* bombers and fighters turning south, away from the enemy—all resulted largely from Nagumo's unexpected change of course from southeast to northeast. It would be idle to speculate on what might have happened had the Japanese admiral continued to close Midway.

APPENDIX
B

~~~~~~~~~~

WHO SANK THE *KAGA*?

IT HAS BEEN suggested that at the time of the dive-bombing attack, *Hiryu* and *Soryu* were to the east of *Akagi* and *Kaga*, with *Hiryu* far out in front of the other ships. However, this is a reversal of the cruising disposition given by Captain Takahisa Amagai, *Kaga's* Air Officer, Captain Susumu Kawaguchi, Air Officer of *Hiryu*, and Captain Taijiro Aoki, *Akagi's* Commanding Officer, which placed *Akagi* and *Kaga* to the eastward.[1] It is therefore not immediately clear why Nagumo would have chosen to shift this original cruising order at the time that he changed course to 070°, unless, afraid of new attacks by Midway-based aircraft, he wished to put his two heavy carriers on the left, or far side, of the formation. However, in the absence of stronger evidence, I am assuming that he held his ships in their original steaming positions, that is, *Akagi* and *Kaga* to the right of *Hiryu* and *Soryu*.

It has also been asserted that Leslie, who started his dive only a minute or two ahead of McClusky, attacked the carrier *Soryu*. It must be noted, however, that the *Soryu*, like the *Hiryu*, was a small carrier, displacing only 10,000 tons, and that the *Akagi* and *Kaga* were much larger, each displacing about 27,000 tons. Moreover, prior to the launching of *Yorktown's* planes, Leslie had studied pictures of the carriers in question and therefore knew perfectly well that the *Akagi*-class was considerably larger than the *Soryu*-class. As he approached his dive position from the southeast he found two carriers below him, one large, the other small, but both potential targets. He chose the large one simply because it was large and was just as accessible as the small one. This was no hasty decision made in the heat of battle —there were no Japanese fighters aloft to molest him since they had all been pulled down to drive off the torpedo attacks. Leslie's vision was clear, he could see plainly that there was an unmistakable difference in the size of the two enemy carriers, and he had sufficient time to compare the two and select the heavier and therefore more valuable one as his target. Furthermore, largely because there was no fighter opposition, Leslie made "a particularly accurate dive," the best he could recall.[2]

It is therefore suggested here that Bombing Squadron Three hit a heavy, not a light, carrier. Assuming for the moment that this is correct, the next question is, which one was it? *Akagi* or *Kaga*? On this point there is some confusion. Leslie himself at first believed that he had attacked the *Kaga*, but after reading more battle reports he concluded that his target must have been the *Akagi*, a view supported by some of his former squadron members.

American naval architects have consistently designed carriers with islands situated on the starboard side, but the Japanese built some of their carriers with port-side islands, a fact which could very well cause confusion in battle reports. How were the islands arranged on the Japanese carriers at Midway? Opposite Page 192 of the Fuchida-Okumiya book there is an excellent photograph of the *Hiryu*, showing her island to port. The 1941 issue of *Jane's Fighting Ships* (Page 293) shows a picture of the *Soryu* with her island on the starboard side but reports that her sister ship *Hiryu* carried her island structure on the port side. On Page 295 of the same *Jane's* there is a photograph of the *Kaga* with a starboard island, but it is noted that her sister ship *Akagi* carried her island on the port side and farther aft. On the same page there is a small insert photograph, unfortunately not too clear, showing the *Akagi* with a port-side island. During his interrogation after the war, Captain Kawaguchi of the *Hiryu* was asked:

"Will you confirm the position of the islands in relation to bow of ship?" He answered: "*Akagi*—port, *Soryu*—starboard, *Kaga*—starboard." [3] Thus both *Jane's* and Captain Kawaguchi confirm that the two large carriers of Nagumo's Striking Force had islands on opposing sides.

Finally the Japanese log carries an entry for 10:43 (7:43 Tokyo time):

"Fighter aboard the *Akagi* to starboard of the bridge catches fire and spreads to bridge . . ." [4]

Although this may be an awkward way of putting it, because of the shortcomings of translation, it is clear that since the aircraft was burning on the starboard (right) side of the *Akagi's* bridge, the bridge structure itself had to be on the port side of the ship.

Leslie's account of the battle, describing quite fully the carrier he attacked, places the bridge island unequivocally on the starboard side. We also know that the *Hiryu*, because she was so far to the north, did not come under attack by either McClusky or Leslie. Therefore, granting that the *Akagi* had a port-side island, the only carriers Bombing Squadron Three (Leslie) could have attacked were *Kaga* or *Soryu*, both with islands to starboard. Yet Leslie did not merely guess that he was attacking a large carrier—he knew it by direct comparison. That carrier had to be the *Kaga*.

Keeping in mind that Leslie began his attack just before McClusky, it is significant that the Japanese log (Page 19) carries the following entry for 10:22 (7:22 Tokyo time):

"*Akagi* sees *Kaga* being dive bombed . . ."

But was the *Akagi* herself already hit? No, for the same entry continues:

"Fighters ordered to take off as soon as readied."

And then the log goes on (Page 20):

10:25 (7:25) "*Akagi* notes fires aboard *Kaga* . . ."
10:26 (7:26) "Three bombers dive on *Akagi* . . ."

The arguments set forth here would not affect McClusky's attack on the *Akagi*—they would, in fact, confirm it, but would change his other target from *Kaga* to *Soryu*. The approximate disposition of Nagumo's carriers at the time of the fatal attack would also have to be rearranged. It is a tedious job, and often a frustrating one, to reconstruct a precise fleet formation at the time of an engagement, and this is especially true of the Battle of Midway since all of Nagumo's carriers were sent to the bottom. However, with some facts and a few moderate suppositions, we can explain some of the tumultuous events which happened with such electrifying speed between 10:20 and 10:30 on the morning of 4 June 1942.

Figure 5 is adapted from the sketch included in Enclosure C of *Yorktown's* Battle Report, showing the relative positions of three carriers as seen by Bombing Squadron Three. The names of the carriers, of course, were not supplied with the original sketch since they were not known at the time of the attack, but the identifying words "large CV" and "small CV" were indicated. *Hiryu* does not appear since, quite literally, she was out of the picture, steaming north at full speed.

Waldron's heroic attack at 9:28 raised havoc with Nagumo's disposition and that of his ships as well. Then with Lindsey's attack dying out before 10 o'clock and Massey's coming to life shortly after, it is not surprising that the enemy force would have been scattered all over the ocean just at the time when McClusky and Leslie arrived with their bombs. To justify the labels I have taken the liberty to apply to Figure 5, I must again refer to the Japanese log. My principal assumption is that Nagumo, despite his frequent harassment by torpedo planes, was trying to keep his ships in approximately the same order they had been in prior to the course change made shortly after 9 o'clock. That would put *Akagi* ahead of *Kaga* on the right side of the formation, *Hiryu* and *Soryu* on the left. Naturally they were not steaming with the militant precision of a pre-war naval review, since they had been engaged in evasive maneuvers.

My reasons for calling the most southerly ship in Figure

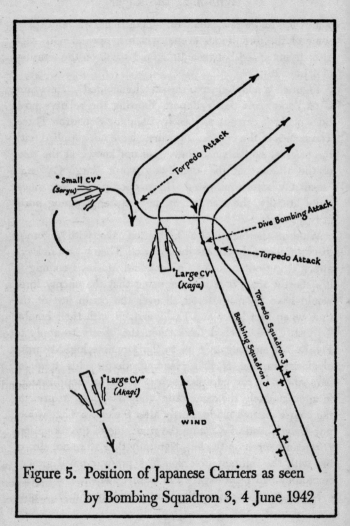

Figure 5. Position of Japanese Carriers as seen
        by Bombing Squadron 3, 4 June 1942

6 (third panel) the *Akagi* are as follows: After Lindsey's attack Nagumo had only about ten or fifteen minutes to get his ships back into some acceptable cruising order, but then Massey rolled in from the southeast. Again the carriers zigzagged, thus breaking their already shabby formation. The Japanese log notes (Page 19) that at 10:11 (7:11) *Akagi* swung around to place the starboard group of torpedo planes to her stern, which would obviously mean a move to the northwest, since Massey was attacking from the southeast. And this appears to be precisely what happened because the 10:14 (7:14) entry in the log finds *Akagi* settling on a course of 300°. *Kaga*, it would appear, kept generally on a northerly course which put her ahead and to the right of the westbound *Akagi* but showed Massey her starboard quarter.

The next significant log entry is the one for 10:20 (7:20). It reads:

"*Akagi* reports sighting bomber bearing 30 degrees directly over *Kaga* and goes into a maximum turn."

From the time she had settled on a course of 300°, *Akagi* had been steaming eastward, presumably at 25 knots or more, for six minutes. This would have moved her about 2.5 miles to the left of the column she had been leading and would have put her almost dead astern of the northbound *Soryu* bringing up the rear of the left column. *Akagi's* bearing of the "bomber," and hence of the *Kaga* directly below it, confirms her own position to the southwest of her sister ship. At the same time she began a maximum turn which—I think it reasonable to assume—was to the south, away from the "bomber." The three panels of Figure 6, based upon the foregoing analysis, show the estimated movements of

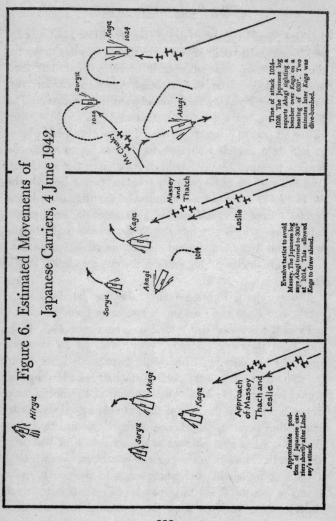

Figure 6. Estimated Movements of
Japanese Carriers, 4 June 1942

Approximate position of Japanese carriers shortly after Lindsey's attack.

Evasive tactics to avoid Massey. The Japanese log says Akagi turned to 300° at 1014. This allowed Kaga to draw ahead.

Time of attack 1024–1026. The Japanese log reports Akagi sighting a bomber over Kaga on a bearing of 030°. Two minutes later Kaga was dive-bombed.

the Japanese carriers as I have envisaged them.

American and Japanese reports on the engagement, of course, are open to many interpretations, but no matter which view prevails in the long run, the Navy's overwhelming victory at Midway will not appear less decisive.

CLIMAX AT MIDWAY:
A CHRONOLOGY
26 MAY—7 JUNE, 1942

26–28 May	Japanese Combined Fleet weighs anchor from Ominato and Hashirajima, Japan, and the islands of Saipan and Guam.
28 May	Admiral Spruance's Task Force Sixteen, flagship *Enterprise* in company with *Hornet*, leaves Pearl Harbor for Point "Luck."
30 May	Admiral Fletcher's Task Force Seventeen, flagship *Yorktown*, leaves Pearl Harbor for Point "Luck." Fletcher in tactical command.
3 June	Japanese invasion transports (Admiral Tanaka) discovered by American reconnaissance aircraft. Tanaka attacked by Army B-17's. No Japanese ships sunk. Aleutian Striking Force (Admiral Kakuta) launches carrier aircraft attack on Dutch Harbor as feint.
4 June (A.M.) Dawn	Admiral Nagumo begins launching first air attack wave for Midway from carriers *Akagi*, *Kaga*, *Hiryu* and *Soryu*. Second wave held in reserve.
4:30	Fletcher, Nagumo and Midway Island Command send off scout planes.
5:34–6:03	PBY's from Midway report enemy carriers approaching the Atoll.

5:53	Midway radar picks up Japanese flight. Midway launches counterattack force of Army, Navy and Marine Corps aircraft in an attempt to halt invasion.
6:07	Fletcher, with search planes in the air, orders Spruance to attack Japanese carriers. Spruance turns SW.
6:35–6:45	Japanese air attack on Midway destroys oil tanks on Sand Island and the powerhouse on Eastern Island.
7:00	Japanese air strike leader, Lieutenant Tomonaga, advises Nagumo that another strike on Midway is necessary. Nagumo hesitates.
7:02	Spruance begins launch of air strike on Nagumo from *Enterprise* and *Hornet*.
7:05	Nagumo attacked by first wave of Midway-based planes, including Army B-26's and Navy TBF's. No hits obtained.
7:15	Nagumo orders second wave, readied for torpedo attack on enemy ships, to change armament to bombs for second strike on Midway. *This is the most critical decision of the battle*.
7:28	Nagumo receives message from Japanese search plane reporting presence of enemy ships to northeast.
7:45	After further hesitation, Nagumo orders attack on American ships by those planes which had not yet been de-armed of torpedoes.
	At same time Nagumo orders search pilot to identify the enemy ships sighted at 7:28.
8:00–8:10	Nagumo attacked by Midway-based Marine Corps and Army bombers. No hits obtained.
8:09	Japanese search plane reports that enemy force composed of only cruisers and destroyers.
8:20	U.S. submarine *Nautilus* attacks Nagumo Force. Misses.
	Yorktown planes take to the air.
	Japanese search plane reports: ENEMY ACCOMPANIED BY WHAT APPEARS TO BE A CARRIER.
8:30	Nagumo sights own first wave of Midway attack planes returning. Decides to recover these aircraft first before launching second attack wave against enemy ships.

Climax At Midway: A Chronology

Admiral Yamaguchi, second in command of Carrier Striking Force, urges Nagumo to launch attack immediately. Nagumo does not concur.

8:37–9:18	Recovery of Japanese aircraft of first wave underway. Nagumo changes course from SE to NNE to attack American carriers.
9:28	Fifteen *Hornet* torpedo planes attack Nagumo. All shot down. No hits obtained.
9:30	Fourteen *Enterprise* torpedo planes attack Nagumo. Ten shot down. No hits obtained.
10:00	Twelve *Yorktown* torpedo planes attack Nagumo. Ten shot down. No hits obtained.
10:00–10:24	Nagumo prepares to launch attack. Flight decks loaded with aircraft. Japanese fighters, having beaten off successive waves of torpedo planes, are at low altitude. First wave of American dive bombers arrive.
10:24	*Yorktown* dive bombers hit *Kaga*.
10:26	*Enterprise* dive bombers hit *Akagi* and *Soryu*.
	(All three Japanese carriers burn. *Hiryu*, farther to the north, escapes this attack.)
10:40	*Hiryu* launches attack on American force.
10:47	Nagumo abandons burning flagship *Akagi*.
11:59	*Yorktown's* radar picks up *Hiryu's* planes approaching from westward. Soon afterward *Yorktown* is bombed.

4 June (P.M.)

12:20	*Yorktown*, smoking, is dead in the water.
12:45	*Hiryu* launches second attack.
1:30	Fletcher shifts flag to cruiser *Astoria*.
1:40	*Yorktown's* damage partially repaired. Underway at 20 knots.
2:42	*Yorktown* hit by second *Hiryu* attack. *Yorktown* again dead in the water after torpedo hit. Dangerous list develops.
3:00	*Yorktown's* captain orders "abandon ship."
3:30	Spruance begins launching attack on the *Hiryu*.
5:00	*Hiryu* hit by Spruance's air attack, bursts into flames.
7:13	*Soryu* sinks.

7:25   *Kaga* sinks.

(During the night of 4–5 June Admiral Spruance re-tires eastward.)

5 June (A.M.)

2:55   Admiral Yamamoto cancels Midway invasion.

3:42   U.S. submarine *Tambor* causes collision of Japanese cruisers *Mogami* and *Mikuma*.

4:55   The burning *Akagi* sunk by Japanese torpedoes.

8:05   Marine Corps aircraft from Midway attack damaged *Mogami* and *Mikuma*. No hits obtained.

9:00   *Hiryu* sinks.

5 June (P.M.)

3:45   *Enterprise* and *Hornet* launch air strikes on retreating Japanese Fleet. Marine pilot, Captain Richard E. Fleming, crashes plane on *Mikuma*. No other hits.

6 June (A.M.)

8:00   *Enterprise* and *Hornet* begin launching first morn-ing attack on retreating cruisers *Mogami* and *Mikuma*.

Second attack launched at 10:45, third at 1:30 p.m. During these attacks both cruisers hit. *Mogami* escapes to Truk; *Mikuma* sinks.

6 June (P.M.)

1:30   Abandoned *Yorktown*, with salvage party on board, torpedoed by Japanese submarine *I-168*. Destroyer *Hammann*, alongside *Yorktown*, sunk by torpedo hit. *Yorktown* now low in water.

(During night of 6–7 June *Yorktown's* list increases.)

7 June (A.M.)

6:00   *Yorktown* sinks. Battle of Midway over.

~~~~~~~~~

BIBLIOGRAPHY

SOME OF the material used in the preparation of this book was derived from discussions with and personal letters from individuals who played a part in the Midway action, and acknowledgments have been made in the Introduction. The bulk of the information, however, came from naval records preserved in the History Division of the Navy Department. The principal unpublished Action Reports utilized for this study were taken from the following commands:

Commander-in-Chief, Pacific Fleet

Commander Task Force Seventeen

Commanding Officer *U.S.S. Yorktown* (including reports of aircraft squadrons attached to his command)

Commanding Officer *U.S.S. Astoria*

Commanding Officer *U.S.S. Portland*

Commander Destroyer Squadron Two (including various reports from the destroyers *Anderson, Hammann, Hughes, Morris* and *Russell*

Commander Task Force Sixteen

Commanding Officer *U.S.S. Enterprise* and

Commanding Officer *U.S.S. Hornet* (including reports of aircraft squadrons attached to their commands)

Commander Cruiser Division Six

Commanding Officer *U.S.S. New Orleans*

Commanding Officer *U.S.S. Vincennes*

Commanding Officer *U.S.S. Pensacola*

Climax At Midway

Reports of various ships attached to Destroyer Squadrons One and Six

Commander Submarine Force, Pacific Fleet, and the reports of various submarines under his command

U.S. Naval Air Station, Midway

Marine Aircraft Group Twenty-Two

There are countless scattered references to the Japanese Navy and the Battle of Midway which, if assembled, would make up a very long but unimpressive bibliography. Therefore I have tried to select certain articles and books which would be of use to anyone wishing to pursue a further study of Japanese naval power and the Midway engagement.

The *United States Naval Institute Proceedings* has published a great many articles on the Japanese Navy, of which the following are especially significant:

James A. Field, Jr., "Admiral Yamamoto," October 1949, p. 1105.

Hajime Fukaya, "Japan's Wartime Carrier Construction," September 1955, p. 1031.

———, "The Shokakus—Pearl Harbor to Leyte Gulf," June 1952, p. 638.

Major Y. Horie (Former Imperial Japanese Army), "The Failure of the Japanese Convoy Escort," October 1956, p. 1073.

Warren S. Howard, "Japanese Destroyers in World War II," January 1952, p. 51.

———, "Japan's Heavy Cruisers in the War," May 1950, p. 533.

Louis Morton, "Japanese Policy and Strategy in Mid-War," February 1959, p. 52.

———, "The Japanese Decision for War," December 1954, p. 1325.

Atsushi Oi, "Why Japan's Anti-Submarine Warfare Failed," June 1952, p. 587.

E. B. Potter, "The Navy's War Against Japan," August 1950, p. 825.

———, "The Japanese Navy Tells Its Story," February 1947, p. 137.

Bibliography

Rear Admiral Logan Ramsey, USN, "The 'Ifs' of Pearl Harbor," April 1950, p. 365.

Walton L. Robinson, "*Akagi*, Famous Japanese Carrier," May 1948, p. 579.

Robert E. Ward, "The Inside Story of the Pearl Harbor Plan," December 1951, p. 1271.

Captain J. C. Wylie, Jr., USN, "Reflections on the War in the Pacific," April 1952, p. 351.

GENERAL PERIODICAL LITERATURE
—— "Battle of Midway," *Time* Magazine, 10 June 1957, p. 26.

J. Bryan, III, "Never a Battle Like Midway," *The Saturday Evening Post*, 26 March 1949, p. 24. This is one of the best short accounts of the action.

Sidney L. James, "Torpedo Squadron 8," *Life* Magazine, 31 August 1942, p. 70.

Fletcher Pratt, "Spruance: Picture of the Admiral," *Harper's* Magazine, August 1946, p. 144.

Lieutenant Commander John S. Thach, USN, "The Red Rain of Battle," *Collier's* Magazine, 5 December 1942, p. 14.

Lloyd Wendt, "The True Story of Heroic Squadron 8," in *Grafic*, the magazine section of the *Chicago Sunday Tribune*. A series of nine articles appearing between 30 May and 25 July 1948.

NAVAL PERIODICAL LITERATURE
—— *Admiral Yamamoto's Yeoman's Story*, a brief account of the battle in possession of the Navy Department. Origin not indicated; of little historical value.

—— *Interrogations of Japanese Officials*, (2 Vols.), United States Strategic Bombing Survey, Naval Analysis Division, 1945.

—— *The Battle of Midway, Aerology and Naval Warfare*, Aerology Section, Chief of Naval Operations, Washington, March 1944. (NAVAER 50-401-1)

———— *The Battle of Midway Including the Aleutian Phase, June 3 to June 14, 1942*. A mimeographed analysis prepared by the U.S. Naval War College, 1948.

———— *The Japanese Story of the Battle of Midway*, Office of Naval Intelligence, Washington, June 1947. There is a May issue of this combined Japanese log but with different pagination.

Lieutenant Colonel Robert D. Heinl, Jr., USMC, *Marines at Midway*, a monograph published by the Division of Public Information, United States Marine Corps, 1948.

BOOKS

Andrieu d'Albas, *Death of a Navy*, Devin-Adair, New York, 1957.

Mitsuo Fuchida and Masatake Okumiya, *Midway, The Battle That Doomed Japan*, Edited by Clarke H. Kawakami and Roger Pineau, Copyright 1955 by the United States Naval Institute.

Mochitsura Hashimoto, *Sunk, The Story of the Japanese Submarine Fleet, 1941–1945*, Henry Holt, New York, 1954.

Ernest J. King and Walter M. Whitehill, *Fleet Admiral King*, W. W. Norton, New York, 1952.

S. E. Morison, *History of United States Naval Operations in World War II*, Vol. IV, Little, Brown and Co., Boston, 1949.

Masatake Okumiya and Jiro Horikoshi (with Martin Caidin), *Zero*, Ballantine, New York, 1956.

Theodore Roscoe, *United States Submarine Operations in World War II*, United States Naval Institute, Annapolis, 1948.

Theodore Taylor, *The Magnificent Mitscher*, W. W. Norton, New York, 1954.

Rear Admiral Robert A. Theobald, USN, *The Final Secret of Pearl Harbor*, Devin-Adair, New York, 1954.

NOTES

Chapter 2

1. See an evaluation of the letter in James A. Field's fine article, "Admiral Yamamoto," in *United States Naval Institute Proceedings*, October, 1949.
2. Captain Watanabe, a member of Admiral Yamamoto's staff, in *Int. Jap. Off.*, Vol. I, p. 66.
3. Mitsuo Fuchida and Masatake Okumiya, *Midway, The Battle That Doomed Japan*, Edited by Clarke H. Kawakami and Roger Pineau, Copyright 1955 by the United States Naval Institute, pp. 68–69.
4. Admiral Crace's views are in answer to my queries to him and were transmitted to me by the Historical Section of the British Admiralty. Admiral Fletcher, who explained shortly after the battle his determination to break up the Port Moresby invasion at all cost, recently reviewed his Coral Sea decisions with me, emphasizing the spirit of cordiality and cooperation which existed between him and Admiral Crace.
5. *Int. Jap. Off.*, Vol., I, p. 30.
6. The overconfident Japanese pilots reported both carriers as sinking; they also mistook the *Lexington* for the *Saratoga*.
7. *Int. Jap. Off.*, Vol. I, pp. 30 and 68.

Chapter 3

1. Fuchida and Okumiya, *op. cit.*, p. 95.
2. *The Japanese Story of the Battle of Midway*, Office of Naval Intelligence, June 1947, p. 3. The May issue of O.N.I. Review carries the same account, but with different pagination.
3. This brief exchange was recorded by an eyewitness, Lieutenant Colonel Robert C. McGlashan, USMC. *Cf.* Robert D. Heinl, *Marines at Midway*, published by the Historical Section of the U.S. Marine Corps, 1948, p. 22.
4. Figures are derived from the Navy Department's documentary film, *The Battle of Midway*. They do not, of course, take into account the vast number of auxiliary ships which were assigned to the operation. The "actual" figures do not agree with information included in Fuchida and Okumiya, *op. cit.*, pp. 251–260. For example, the three light carriers attached to the commands of Yamamoto, Fujita and Kakuta are omitted.

5. For a fine portrayal of Admiral Spruance, see Fletcher Pratt's article, "Spruance: Picture of the Admiral," in *Harper's* Magazine, August, 1946, p. 144.

6. *Int. Jap. Off.*, Vol. II, p. 465. Fuchida and Okumiya, *op. cit.*, p. 120, indicate that two ships were sighted.

7. S. E. Morison, *History of U.S. Naval Operations in World War II*, Vol. IV, p. 94, indicates that the arrival of the submarines on station on 3 June "was supposed to be in good time" to catch any American forces moving out of Pearl Harbor, since Yamamoto expected a tardy reaction from Nimitz. The Japanese authorities, Fuchida and Okumiya, *op. cit.*, p. 142, assert that the submarines arrived on patrol two days late! There is also a minor discrepancy with respect to the exact location of the patrol. Compare Fuchida and Okumiya, p. 87, and Captain Watanabe in *Int. Jap. Off.*, Vol. I, p. 67.

8. Watanabe, *ibid.*

CHAPTER 4

1. *Tambor, Dolphin, Trout, Gato, Grayling, Grenadier, Cachalot, Nautilus, Grouper, Flying Fish* and *Gudgeon*.

2. *Trigger, Narwhal* and *Plunger*.

3. *Growler, Finback, Pike* and *Tarpon*.

4. For a complete account of submarine warfare during World War II, see the highly readable work of Theodore Roscoe, *United States Submarine Operations in World War II*, U.S. Naval Institute, Annapolis, 1949. A slightly abridged but nonetheless useful pocketbook edition has appeared under the title, *Pigboats*, Bantam Books, New York, 1958.

5. Information from Captain (then Lieutenant) E. D'H. Haskins, who was executive officer of the *Flying Fish*.

6. *U.S.S. Hornet's* Battle Report.

7. Destroyer Squadron One—*Phelps, Worden, Monaghan* and *Aylwin;* Destroyer Squadron Six—*Balch, Conyngham, Benham, Ellet* and *Maury*.

8. *U.S.S. Hornet's* Battle Report.

9. Theodore Taylor, *The Magnificent Mitscher*, W. W. Norton, New York, 1954, p. 127.

10. Weather information submitted by the ships engaged in the battle was often contradictory. The aerological data presented in this study is derived largely from a careful analysis made by the Navy: *The Battle of Midway, Aerology and Naval Warfare*, NAVAER 50-401-1, of March 1944.

11. *U.S.S. Enterprise's* Battle Report.

12. *The Japanese Story of the Battle of Midway*, p. 6.

13. Fuchida and Okumiya, *op. cit.*, p. 117.

14. During the afternoon of 2 June the fog was so thick that usual ship-to-ship signalling was impossible and Nagumo was forced to use his radio to order a course change, a fact which caused him some worry. He need not have been distressed by this exigent violation of radio silence, for neither Fletcher nor Spruance intercepted his tactical message.

Notes

15. *U.S.S. Yorktown's* Battle Report.

16. These messages are taken from the *Enterprise's* action report since part of *Yorktown's* tactical message file must have gone down with the ship, as did many of her papers. Her log accidentally fell into the sea while being transferred from the carrier to an awaiting raft. See Captain Buckmaster's report on the loss of his ship, dated 17 June 1942. However, the Communications section of *Yorktown's* Battle Report indicates that Admiral Fletcher's dispatch file, of which these messages were presumably a part, was taken from the sinking ship and transferred to Pearl Harbor. In any event, Fletcher's subsequent action leaves no doubt that he received the contact messages at the same time that Spruance did.

17. The principal sources used for the balance of the action narrative are the battle reports of Commander Task Force Seventeen (Fletcher); Commander Task Force Sixteen (Spruance); *U.S.S. Yorktown; U.S.S. Enterprise; U.S.S. Hornet;* U.S. Naval Air Station, Midway; Preliminary Report of Marine Air Group-22; *The Japanese Story of the Battle of Midway; U.S. Strategic Bombing Survey, Naval Analysis Division, Interrogation of Japanese Officials;* and the reports of various subordinate air and surface commands, all of which source material is cited in full in the bibliography.

CHAPTER 5

1. Heinl, *op. cit.,* p. 27, indicates that an "insoluble contradiction prevents positive knowledge of how many fighters" the Marines got off the ground that day. But it was certainly no more than twenty-six, and then only five of these—the F4F-3 "Wildcats"—were any match for the Japanese Zero.

2. Heinl, *op. cit.,* p. 42, credits the Marine pilots with downing twenty-five enemy bombers and eighteen fighters, and the Marine gunners at Midway with at least ten more. Admiral Nimitz credited the Marine batteries with ten Japanese aircraft, while the air officer of the Japanese carrier *Hiryu* claimed that ten planes were lost from his ship alone. But Fuchida, who was on board the *Akagi* when the returning aircraft were recovered, says only six failed to return. Cf. Fuchida and Okumiya, *op. cit.,* p. 157.

3. Captain Glidden claimed to have seen "two hits and one miss that was right alongside the bow." Heinl, *op. cit.,* p. 35, asserts that these hits were confirmed by Captain Taijiro Aoki, *Akagi's* commanding officer. Aoki (in *Int. Jap. Off.,* Vol. I, p. 14) does mention two bomb hits "by dive bombing about two hours after sunrise," but his time is obviously wrong since sunrise on the 4th occurred at about 5 o'clock. He explains further that these two bomb hits were fatal to the *Akagi.* "Engines were helpless, fire damage, could not navigate so gave up the ship. . . ." Yet, when the *Akagi* was hit with carrier-based planes more than two hours after Henderson's heroic attack she was maneuvering at high speed with no signs of damage. Fuchida disclaims any hits on Nagumo's force by this or any other shore-based planes. (Fuchida and Okumiya, *op. cit.,* p. 163). Yet the Japanese log (*O.N.I. Review,* May 1947) mentions that

at 0810 (0510 Tokyo time) bomb hits on *Akagi* and *Hiryu* were noted. These were probably near misses, or at least not damaging hits, for *Hiryu's* planes later in the day were able to bomb the *Yorktown*. It is also certain that the two hits Aoki claims crippled the *Akagi* were actually delivered by carrier-based aircraft.

Even so, Henderson's dive bombers helped to push Nagumo off balance, and their desperate flight, undertaken that day against impossible odds, deserves an honored place in the history of naval warfare.

4. Fuchida and Okumiya, *op. cit.*, p. 170.
5. This is, of course, 8 a.m. for this narrative. Nagumo's "5 a.m." is in Tokyo time.

CHAPTER 6

1. This was only part of the squadron. Six planes had been temporarily stationed at Midway and attacked the Japanese ships from there. Five of these were lost.
2. Based on information from George Gay, these words introduce a departure in our generally accepted version of the Battle of Midway, which argues that Waldron flew southwest, missed the Japanese ships at the expected point of contact, and then turned sharply to the north in order to attack them. After reviewing numerous action reports and discussing the matter with several veterans of the battle, I was led to the conclusion that Waldron did not make any sharp changes in his original course but rather set out on a more or less straight line for the Japanese formation. Since my arguments for this "different" version of the battle are too lengthy for a footnote, I have included them in Appendix A.
3. Based on a statement by Leroy Quillen, ARM 3C, USN, who was with Bombing Squadron Eight. "I am quite sure it was Lieutenant Commander Waldron's voice," he said, "as I have heard it on the air many times." *U.S.S. Hornet's* Battle Report.
4. Since he was not immediately rescued, Gay was able to watch the remainder of the battle. That night he inflated his life raft and climbed into it, and on the following morning an American patrol plane signalled that it had seen him, proceeded on its assigned mission and later returned to pick him up. He was the only one left of *Hornet's* Torpedo Squadron Eight, but the courage which Waldron had given to his men remained with him. When asked by a doctor at Pearl Harbor what he had done for his wounds, Gay was able to reply with a smile that he had soaked them in salt water for many hours.
5. Much of the material for the remainder of Chapter 6 is taken from *U.S.S. Yorktown* Battle Report.

CHAPTER 7

1. This portion of the narrative is based on information derived from battle reports of the *U.S.S. Yorktown* and Bombing Squadron Three, the Jap-

Notes

anese Log (*The Japanese Story of the Battle of Midway*, O.N.I., June 1947) and facts provided by Rear Admiral Leslie and Captain Paul A. Holmberg. My interpretation of events does not agree in all respects with previous accounts of the battle. The arguments which I offer in support of my version of the action are contained in Appendix B.

2. The following description of the attack on the *Yorktown* is derived from Captain Buckmaster's Battle Report and information from Joseph H. Adams, a yeoman on Admiral Fletcher's staff, who was then stationed on the port catwalk and witnessed the attack from there.

3. Fuchida and Okumiya, *op. cit.*, p. 192. The Japanese log, however, reports that at 1 p.m. (10 o'clock Tokyo time) a *Yorktown* pilot, fished from the sea, informed the Japanese that the American force was made up of the *Yorktown*, *Enterprise* and *Hornet*. Cf., *The Japanese Story of the Battle of Midway*, (O.N.I., June 1947), p. 24.

CHAPTER 8

1. *The Japanese Story of the Battle of Midway*, (O.N.I.), June 1947, p. 27.

2. Air Operations Officer's Report, *U.S.S. Hornet*, and *The Japanese Story of the Battle of Midway*, p. 30.

3. *The Japanese Story . . . , ibid.*

4. Heinl, *op. cit.*, p. 39.

5. It appears there were two Engineer Commanders on board the *Hiryu*. The interrogation of Japanese prisoners, part of Admiral Nimitz's report of 28 June, lists a Commander Eiso as chief engineer. *The Japanese Story of the Battle of Midway*, p. 9, lavishes praise on Commander Aimune, "down to the last man," which would lead one to believe that he was the chief engineer.

6. Quoted in Fuchida and Okumiya, *op. cit.*, pp. 197–8.

7. Quoted in Andrieu d'Albas's *Death Of A Navy*, p. 134.

8. Knowing now that Captain Kaku went down with his ship, it is curious that these survivors, when questioned later, expressed disgust that he left the *Hiryu* while they were still on board. Since none of them reported seeing either Yamaguchi or Kaku standing on the bridge, one might speculate as to whether or not both men committed hara-kiri sometime before the *Hiryu* sank.

9. *The Japanese Story of the Battle of Midway*, p. 34. "AF," as we have learned earlier, was the Japanese Navy's cryptographic symbol for Midway Island.

10. Quoted in Fuchida and Okumiya, *op. cit*, p. 214.

11. Transmitted at 11:40 p.m. and midnight. *The Japanese Story of the Battle of Midway*, p. 36.

12. Quoted in Fuchida and Okumiya, *op. cit.*, p. 217.

CHAPTER 9

1. War Diary, Third War Patrol, *U.S.S. Tambor* (SS 198), and information from Edward D. Spruance, now Captain, USN.

Climax At Midway

2. Captain (later Rear Admiral) Soji, in *Int. Jap. Off.*, II, p. 363.
3. *Ibid.* For his feat Fleming was posthumously awarded the Medal of Honor. Moreover, his daring dive apparently caused far more damage to the *Mikuma* than had previously been believed, for his sacrificial crash caused an intense explosion which killed all hands in the starboard engine room. *Cf.* Fuchida and Okumiya, *op. cit.*, p. 226.
4. This portion of the narrative is based generally on Admiral Spruance's Battle Report.
5. The figures are taken from Buckmaster's account. *Hammann's* report, however, indicates that there were only 130 enlisted men in the salvage party.
6. These were *Balch, Benham, Gwin, Hughes* and *Monaghan*, the last of which was sent by Spruance. *Hammann*, of course, remained alongside.
7. 6:52 (3:52 Tokyo Time.) *The Japanese Story of the Battle of Midway*, p. 38.
8. For an account of this and other submarine actions, see Mochitsura Hashimoto's *Sunk, The Story of the Japanese Submarine Fleet, 1941–1945.*
9. Kimbrell was recommended for a posthumous award of the Navy Cross for his bravery.
10. Of the B-17's which unsuccessfully searched for the *Mikuma* and *Mogami*, two did not return. Army Major General C. L. Tinker, who led a group of Liberators to bomb Japanese-held Wake Island, himself disappeared in flight.

Appendix A

1. This is Enclosure "A" to the report of *Enterprise's* Commanding Officer, dated 13 June 1942.
2. Action Report, *U.S.S. Hornet.*
3. *Ibid.*, which says that Waldron flew at 100 knots below the clouds, while the remainder of the group flew at 110 knots, climbing to 19,000 feet.
4. *The Japanese Story of the Battle of Midway*, p. 17.
5. Sidney L. James, "Torpedo Squadron 8," *Life*, 31 August 1942.
6. Lloyd Wendt, "The True Story of Heroic Squadron 8," in *Grafic*, the magazine section of the *Chicago Sunday Tribune* from 30 May to 25 July 1948. See especially the installment for 18 July, p. 10.
7. Action Report, Commander, Fighting Squadron Six.
8. The sighting time of 9:30 is reported in Fuchida and Okumiya, *op. cit.*, p. 175.

Appendix B

1. *Int. Jap. Off.*, Vol. I, pp. 1, 4 and 13.
2. Information from Rear Admiral Maxwell F. Leslie, USN (Ret.).
3. *Int. Jap. Off.*, Vol. I, p. 5.
4. *The Japanese Story of the Battle of Midway*, p. 20.

INDEX

Index

Index

Index

Index